SYSTEMA PARADOXA

ACCOUNTS OF CRYPTOZOOLOGICAL IMPORT

VOLUME 18

DAYLIGHT COMES

A TALE OF THE DWAYYO

AS ACCOUNTED BY JOHN L. FRENCH

NEOPARADOXA

Pennsville, NJ

2023

PUBLISHED BY
NeoParadoxa
A division of eSpec Books
PO Box 242
Pennsville, NJ 08070
www.especbooks.com

ISBN: 978-1-956463-39-2
ISBN (ebook): 978-1-956463-38-5

Interior Design: Danielle McPhail
www.sidhenadaire.com

Cover Art: Jason Whitley
Cover Design: Mike and Danielle McPhail, McP Digital Graphics
Interior Illustration: Jason Whitley

Copyediting: Greg Schauer

DEDICATION

TO MY DEAR FRIEND,
BARB SCHUMAN

Author's Note

This story was initially inspired by the story of the Beast of Gevaudan and the similarities between the dwayyo. More information on the Beast of Gevaudan can be found at the end of this tale.

PROLOGUE

By the light of the waning moon, the dwayyo met. Ulf, the pack leader, called the gathering. The adults present sensed this was a solemn occasion, and so none growled, snapped, or fought for a place of dominance. The cubs, on the other hand, had no sense of solemnity or occasion. They ignored the adults and played their usual games of hiding and finding, chasing and mock battle, or the hunting of insects. Of the youths, the older dway who had not yet mated, some watched the cubs and wished they dared join in the play. Others watched and scented each other and wondered about the mysteries of the coming season.

But quiet descended over the pack. Shuffling ceased as Ulf mentally urged them into silence. The youths stopped looking at one another, and even the cubs calmed.

One other joined in that silence. One with the pack, but not of it. One smaller than the dway with no fur to keep him warm. No claws or teeth to kill prey or defend himself. He was a human known by the pack as "Reilly," although he did not use that name anymore. He had been summoned by Ulf, and so he came. It was right for him to be there, for he had guided them to this place and he had given Ulf the warning.

The dwayyo could voice growls and snarls, whines and whimpers, howls and moans. But they spoke to one another mind to mind. This mental ability they also used to terrify prey and make it hesitate long enough to be caught, killed, and eaten.

Many seasons ago, Ulf sent to her followers, *our people, our pack, left our den in the trees of the mountain and journeyed to this place. We did so because the leader of that time chose to involve the pack in the affairs of men. It was a poor choice and nearly led to the end of the pack. This leader's name we have chosen to forget. To maintain the pack, Naester, the new leader, left the mountain and began the search for a new place for our den. He was guided by the human Reilly who led us here. It is a good place with deer, horses, foxes, and other food. Even, if Reilly will forgive, the occasional human.*

From his place outside of the pack circle, the man called Reilly heard the "huh, huh, huh" that served as laughter among the dway. He was sensitive to the thoughts of the dway, always had been, and he knew why they laughed. He smiled his own amusement, feeling safe among them. Had they wanted to eat him they would have done so seasons ago.

We thank you, Reilly, and for your service we grant you the honor of the pack.

The pack turned toward him, acknowledging and agreeing with Ulf's words. Her thanks surprised him. The honor of the pack meant first feeding off prey after the leader and first choice of mate following the alpha male. Reilly nodded and sent his gratitude but he liked his meat cooked and as for the other, he had never even considered it.

Change is coming, Ulf sent, again claiming the attention of the pack. *When Naester led the pack here, it was small and weak. By the time he left the pack, it had grown. Yoke then led and left the pack. Now I lead, and we are as large and as strong as we ever were. And while that is a good thing it is also a problem.*

Reilly had seen this problem first. On the night of the hidden moon, he had called to Ulf and she came, meeting halfway between his home and her den.

As at his first meeting with the dwayyo, Reilly was in awe of her. Her kind were upright wolf-like creatures with claws the size of fighting knives and teeth that could tear anything smaller than an elephant to shreds. Ulf at six-foot was not the tallest dway, nor was she the strongest but she was the fiercest and smartest, and so she ruled the pack.

They met in a clearing close to the road where Reilly parked.

You called, friend Reilly?

I did, Pack Leader. It is about the pack. It is large and strong, so large that soon it will not be able to hide. Already there is talk among my kind of monsters who live on the island of horses, monsters that kill.

We are those monsters?

Yes, and the bodies of some humans taken by the pack have also been found. People are getting a little scared. What we humans fear we kill.

We are stronger than humans.

Reilly sensed the doubt in her mind. She knew as well as he that the pack was not stronger than an army of humans. And with the war over, a small army would be exactly what hunted them.

The pack must survive, he thought to her. *To do so, it must separate as it once did long ago. One part can remain here. Lying low, being careful, becoming a story with which to scare the young to sleep. The rest can go elsewhere, maybe back to the mountain.*

Is it safe to do so?

The fliers sleep. Men have forgotten you. It is safer than here.

Thank you, friend Reilly. I will consider it.

They parted.

Now, at the gathering of the waning moon, Ulf showed how much she had considered it.

The pack has grown too large, she sent to those she led. *It is time for a new one. Choose two leaders. One to return the new pack to the mountain. The other to lead this one.*

This caused some excitement among the dwayyo.

Will you not lead us, Ulf? asked Gunnrr, a seven-foot, black-furred dway. *Either here or to the mountain?*

No, she replied not only to Gunnrr but to the pack as a whole. *I feel within me a sickness. Soon I will leave the pack. Choose your new leaders and choose wisely.*

Ulf withdrew. The pack shared their thoughts without her. They included the youths in this, as when they became adults, they would be led by whoever was chosen.

As the pack decided, Ulf stood apart from it, beside Reilly.

They chose Revna, a brown and grey-furred female — strong, fierce, and equal in height to Ulf. As first chosen, she decided to lead the new pack to the mountain. Next was Gunnrr. He would remain and lead those who did not leave.

Once the leaders were chosen, she turned to Reilly and thought, *Thank you for all you have done. Will you be returning to the mountain?*

Reilly thought of his current life. Rejected by the Army and the Navy, he had served his country as a coast watcher. That was how he had met Rita. She knew him under his real name Sean Meadows. Her husband was one of the first to go overseas and one of the first to die. A year after she received notice from the Army, she invited the man she knew as Sean into her home and her bed.

Reilly shook his head. *My home is here.*

Ulf nodded in understanding, then went to where Gunnrr and Revna stood.

I have no wish to be a burden to the pack, she told them. *Nor do I wish to die alone and in pain.* Having said this, she bared her throat.

Two sets of claws lashed out. Blood spurted from her neck as she fell and died.

The pack, two packs now, gathered around Ulf's fallen body. Ceremoniously they each took a lap of her blood and a bite from her flesh so that she would always be with the pack. Then they left what remained of the body to the lesser predators and scavengers, for it was no longer Ulf.

Having witnessed the end of Ulf, Sean Meadows had a brief word with Revna and then decided he was done with the dwayyo. He turned and walked away from the gathering. No longer would he be Reilly.

Gunnrr and those dwayyo staying behind faded away, leaving Revna with her new pack. *It is still dark. We hunt and feed, then we will sleep. Tomorrow we will leave for the mountain. The man called Reilly showed me in my mind how to travel there. But be quick. Daylight comes.*

Chapter One

The war was over. VE Day and VJ Day had come and passed. People began to feel safe again. Fears of German bombers, Italian submarines, and Japanese invasions faded. The blackouts were gone and while life was not fully back to normal it was heading that way. Hope was returning and people began planning, now that they knew there was going to be a future.

But not for all.

Whatever future Patricia Joseph might have had ended sometime after the troops began to come home. A brunette in her mid-twenties, she'd held a factory job during the war. With demobilization in full swing, her foreman told her to brush up on her secretarial skills since "the boys" would need the work.

"Of course, there may be positions available for some of you gals," the foreman said. He was a nasty sort named Douglas (call me "Dougie") Skinner, all hands and leers. The women who worked the floor knew not to be alone with him, not if they didn't want to be felt up and pinched. On her last day, Skinner cornered Patricia when she left the women's locker room following a break.

"You seem to have the right qualifications." As he said this Skinner openly looked her up and down, making it clear what he thought her "qualifications" were. "In fact, I can think of several positions you'd be good at." His hand found her shoulder. "Maybe we can step into my office and try some out."

When Skinner's hand left Patricia's shoulder and headed south she forcefully tendered her resignation, ramming a knee between his legs. He doubled over and she went back into the locker room to gather her things. As she walked past the still-moaning Skinner, he yelled, "You bitch," and made a grab for her. This time she kicked him in the knee.

When he hit the floor hard, she stepped over his body. "By the way, *Dougie*, I quit."

First shift was less than half over when Patricia Joseph left the plant for the last time. At 3 a.m., the sun was not ready to start shining down on Harbor City. It was dark, and the bus stop stood empty. Patricia normally caught the 8:30 bus. She had no idea how the buses ran this early in the morning, or if they ran at all.

"Maybe I should go back inside…" she said to the air. "Maybe if I pretend nothing happened, ole Doug will too."

Naw. Patricia knew better than that, given she'd hurt more than just Skinner's pride. A smile crept across her face at the thought of how he went down. How often had one of the other girls told her, *"He'd get me alone and…"*? Patricia had heard the stories and didn't want to find out if they were true. She was safer on the bench at the bus stop, safer alone in the dark on an empty street in Harbor City than in that factory.

"At least," she told herself, "it's only Monday, so I only lost a day's pay. And at least I have my lunch."

Patricia placed her lunch pail on the bench beside her. It had been her brother's before he was called to duty. Running her fingers gently over the lid, she opened it, revealing a thermos of coffee, a cheese sandwich, and a butterscotch Krimpet. Next, she took a paperback Agatha Christie novel from her purse. She might as well make the most of however long she had to wait.

Fifteen minutes went by as she ate her lunch and read her book. Engrossed as Patricia was in *The Mysterious Affair at Styles*, she did not hear the growling until it was too late.

CHAPTER TWO

Theodore Syn's desk occupied the back corner of the detective's office. It was battered and scratched up, one drawer was constantly stuck, and none of the legs were of the same length. An old and mostly unread copy of the Harbor City PD procedure manual kept it from wobbling.

Fair enough, Syn thought when he first saw it. He knew the rules, the new guy gets the worst desk, and despite having been in law enforcement for over twenty years, he was the new guy in the Homicide Unit.

Syn had been a patrol cop in Baltimore. After that, he did some freelancing before becoming a detective (*the* detective) in Corbet County, just south of Harbor City. What happened there involved gangsters, roadhouses, strange events, and even stranger creatures. After briefly serving as the county's marshal, he went private again. He spent the war dealing with matters he could not discuss. Suffice it to say that the strange and the weird tended to follow Theodore Syn around.

With the war being over and his government assignment at an end, Syn needed a job. He couldn't afford to go back to private troubleshooting. During the war, he had gotten married and took in his brother's son Jericho, whose parents had been killed by a drunk driver. Syn's wife Cara welcomed the boy and treated him so well that while Syn would always be "Uncle Ted," within six months, Jericho called Cara "Ma."

As the new guy, Syn got the cases no one else wanted to handle — the questionable deaths, the suicides, the dead-end murders with little to no chance of a quick closure. That was okay with him. It was routine work, and after everything he'd been through, what Syn wanted most was routine.

Like this case he was wrapping up. Ray Powers, a drunken high school student, had fallen from a great height during a late-night party held at a pavilion in Greenwood Park. Sitting on a stone wall, chugging the last beer he would ever drink, Powers leaned a bit too far back and lost what little balance he'd had left. Death was instantaneous on impact with the hard ground thirty feet below. Three of Powers' fellow students saw him fall. All three swore that no one was near him when he did. For Syn, it was case closed by accidental death. He would forward the file to the DA's office in case Powers' bereaved parents demanded that "action be taken." If they were rich or important enough, it just might be.

"Syn." The voice belonged to Detective Adam Lynch. Not a polite "Detective Syn" or a friendly "Ted." Just "Syn." Lynch was like that, full of self-importance which he tried to build at the expense of others.

Syn looked up. "Yes, how can I help you?" he asked with a smile.

"No, Syn, you can't help me. The Lieutenant wants to see you, probably another dead high school kid." Lynch said this in a way that implied that was all Syn was good for.

Dropping his case folder in the out bin, Syn stood, said, "Thanks," and went to see Lieutenant Jack Fuller.

When Syn was gone, Lynch was confronted by Detective Jane Higgins.

Higgins was as rare a creature as those Theodore Syn had faced in the mountains of Corbet County and the waters of the Chesapeake Bay. She was a police detective, the first and so far only female detective in the HCPD. Before the war, she had been a policewoman, limited to searching and guarding female prisoners, handling administrative work too sensitive to be done by civilians, and working decoy duty when a woman was required. When a large number of the force had been called up, she saw her chance and took it, becoming first a police officer and later a detective.

"What do you have against the Scarecrow?" Higgins asked him in an interrogatory tone.

"Who?" Lynch asked, not picking up on the fact that he was being questioned as if he was a suspect.

"Syn. That's what they call him. Haven't you noticed — tall, lean, his blonde hair always needing combing? You treat him like he shouldn't be here."

"He shouldn't. Spent the war over here, some kind of government job. Not overseas like some of us." Lynch was a veteran of the European Theater. He was discharged early due to injuries that left him with scars he never showed to anyone. "Probably used his connections to get this job."

Higgins laughed. She had an attractive laugh. It did not go with the rest of her. Her reddish-brown hair was cut short to give the people she arrested less chance of grabbing it. (A lesson learned on her third day of patrol.) She wore women's trouser suits similar to those worn by male detectives. Her only make-up was a touch of lipstick. She dressed not to impress but rather to blend in. If she had a social life, she did not talk about it, preferring to keep it separate from her professional one.

"Theodore Syn already fought his war, the first one. He lied about his age to enlist. Came out of it with a Silver Star and the *Croix de Guerre*. After that, it's said he singlehandedly stopped the Roadhouse War of Corbet County. And someone called 'the Scarecrow' supposedly ran with the masks in the late thirties."

"How do you know this?"

"I'm a detective just like you. And a good detective investigates before she comes to a conclusion about a person."

If Detective Higgins expected Lynch to look chastened, she was disappointed. She changed the subject. "So, how is your Beast case coming?"

"You know I hate that name."

"Too bad. You should know by now once the press names 'em you're stuck with it."

Chapter Three

The Beast. That's what the papers were calling the killer targeting young women on the streets of Harbor City. Three so far. All young, all pretty, all taken when alone. Patricia Joseph had been the first. Followed by Ellen Davis. She had been killed coming home from a date—a late dinner and an even later movie. Her boyfriend, Cliff Moss, had offered to walk her to her door but she told him not to be silly, dashing his hopes of being invited inside. So, he dropped her off and watched her go up her front walk, then, as he described it, "something large and dark" attacked and savaged her. According to the statement Moss gave the police, he immediately ran to help her but she was dead by the time he reached the front step. The truth was Moss just watched, frozen in terror, until the thing ran off then waited until he was sure it wasn't coming back. He'd thought about just driving off but instead went to her aid. His screaming alerted the neighbors who called the police.

Rosie Donovan was the last (so far). She wasn't coming home from a date when she was killed. Rosie had been on the streets since she was fifteen and did what she needed to get by. The night she died she was working the car trade. She had been picked up by Corey Melton, one of her regulars, who came to her for something his wife wouldn't do. He drove her to their usual spot by the docks. He paid her, she did the thing, he thanked her, and she returned to her corner.

She never made it.

"You sure they're connected?" Theodore Syn asked Lieutenant Fuller as the two old friends sat across a desk only less battered than Syn's. He and Fuller had been beat cops together in Baltimore, walking adjoining posts. They kept in touch even after Syn had been fired for daring to arrest a city councilman for murder. While he didn't know all the specifics, Fuller knew more than most about Syn's work in Corbet

County and for the government. It was Jack Fuller who helped get Syn his appointment to the HCPD then fought to get him on his homicide team.

"You have to ask, Scarecrow? Hell, I guess you do. But yeah, they're connected. Lynch caught the first one, the Joseph girl. Thought he had a solid suspect in the foreman, a jerk named Skinner. Someone at the plant saw him make a move on her. She kneed him, decked him, then quit. Lynch figured him good for it, you know, his pride got hurt so he'd hurt her. But the attack …"

Fuller's head shook, then his body shivered as he thought back to the ferocity of the killing. "Too brutal. If she'd been beaten or stabbed, or if he forced himself on her, yeah, I'd put him top of the list. He stayed Lynch's favorite until the Davis girl got it and the ME said the same weapon, or weapons, caused her death. Which let her boyfriend and the third girl's client off the hook."

"So, you've got a thrill killer on your hands?"

"*We've* got one on our hands. You're part of this squad now, Scarecrow. Remember?"

"Yeah, and thanks for that. But I thought Lynch had them?"

"He does. You know the drill, you catch the first, you get the rest."

"So, what do you want from me?"

Even as he asked the question, the Scarecrow thought he knew the answer. He thought about another of the rules of police work — "Do a job once and it's yours." There was a job he'd done more than once and he had a feeling he was being asked to do it again.

Fuller pushed out from his desk, stood, and walked over to a file cabinet. The top drawer screeched when he opened it. He drew out a bottle of Pikesville Rye and two glasses. The drawer screeched again as it closed. Fuller sat and poured them each a drink. Glasses raised in a silent toast; they drank. When the glasses were empty, Fuller said,

"I heard something about you and the Roadhouse Wars, something about monsters. Later I heard about something big swimming in the Chesapeake. Your name got mentioned again. When you called me about a job, I did some checking. Called around. I must have called around too much because I got a personal call from a General Cain who told me to just hire you and stop asking 'so many damned questions.' There was an implied 'or else.' So, Scarecrow, old friend to old friend, one cop to another, what's really in the mountains of Corbet County?"

Another round of drinks was poured. When they were mostly finished, Syn said, "Flying things called snallygasters. Think a bird-lizard mix with a twenty-foot wingspan. On the ground, there were the dwayyo. Big, bad wolves that walk upright and hunt in packs. Both top predators that see men as either annoyances or food. The snallys are mostly gone now. The dway, well, as far as I know, they left and went elsewhere."

That was as much as Syn was willing to tell his friend. He did not see the need to mention that he had blood ties with certain snallygasters. Or that he had once fought and killed dwayyo who had threatened his "cousin's" chicks.

Fuller finished his drink. He looked at the bottle, thought about a third, and decided against it. "And that thing in the bay, what do you call that?"

Syn smiled and shrugged. "I call her Chessie, she calls me Scarecrow."

Fuller's mouth dropped open. He closed it to ask, "Are you shitting me?"

The stare the Scarecrow gave him told him that he was not.

"Jack, what's this all about?"

"Scarecrow, I want you to look into this 'Beast' case. Separate from Lynch."

That usually wasn't done, one detective going behind another. Syn didn't like it but orders were orders, even when they came from old friends. "Why? What's wrong with Lynch, other than he's an arrogant SOB?"

"Yeah, he is. But he's a very good arrogant SOB who closes most of his cases the right way, with good witnesses and solid evidence. But this case ..."

"What about it?"

"Scarecrow, there's a chance the killer isn't human."

When Fuller handed Syn his copy of the case folders and photos from the crime scenes, he told him, "Make sure Lynch doesn't see these. He's a good investigator. I don't want him to think I don't trust him."

"Don't worry, Jack. I'll go over them at home. Cara's used to it and Jericho wants to be a cop. Maybe seeing the photos will change his mind."

"How's Jerry doing?"

"Jericho. He hates the name Jerry. And better. Adjusting. Maybe that's where the whole 'being a cop' thing came from."

Fuller smiled. "And, of course, 'Uncle Ted' had nothing to do with it. They ever find the drunk that killed his parents?"

Theodore's eyes narrowed and his face darkened. "No, and they never will."

The way he said this scared Fuller a little. As if the Scarecrow knew for sure that the drunk driver would never be found and knew why that was. But the lieutenant was a cop, one who knew about "unofficial justice" and the value one places on family.

Syn went home early. Over dinner with his family he talked, mostly to his nephew, about the dead boy in the park, explaining to Jericho that one could sometimes tell if a body had fallen or was thrown from a great height by the distance it landed from the place from which it fell. He didn't say anything about the case folders and photos he brought home.

After dinner, "Jericho, you help Cara clear and with the dishes. I'll be in the study probably most of the evening."

Cara smiled and shook her head but like Syn had told Fuller, she was used to it. "If you finish early enough," she said, "be sure to wake me up for a good night kiss." Her tone implied that more than a kiss might be involved.

The desk in Syn's study was much better than the one in the Homicide office. It was not scratched, nor did the legs wobble. Best of all, it was not near a not-quite-closable window or under a heat vent. And it had a desk lamp that Syn knew would not shock him when he turned it on.

Under the light of that lamp Syn first reviewed the police reports. They did not tell him anything he didn't already know. The dead women did not seem to have been chosen but were victims of opportunity. Nor were they connected in any way, other than being young and female. That suggested to Syn that a human killer might be involved. A non-human predator would not care about the gender of its next meal. Maybe there were male victims who had not yet been found. Maybe the predator preferred women over men. Syn knew of a snallygaster that liked the taste of cows over goats and the taste of humans not at all. Maybe…

But no, Syn decided. It was too soon into this case to start worrying about maybes. He'd read the reports, gather the facts, and go from there.

Nothing from the crime-scene people. No weapons, no usable trace evidence. All the blood samples came back to the victims' types.

The Medical Examiner's report was only a little more helpful. In each case, multiple lacerations were observed in several areas on the victim's body. These lacerations consisted of four parallel cuts of near equal length. These cuts maybe have been caused by a multi-bladed weapon although animal attack should not be ruled out. Death was due to exsanguination.

The autopsy report on Ellen Davis noted that her wounds were similar to those found on Patricia Joseph. Likewise, that of Rosie Donovan were similar to those of the first two victims. The addendum to the last report was interesting:

Bone sections bearing laceration marks were removed from the subject's body and preserved. It is recommended that the bodies of subjects Joseph and Davis be exhumed and similar sections be taken from each of their bodies and any bone markings found be compared to those from subject Donovan. Appropriate sectioning will be done should any further subjects arrive with similar wounds.

This Dela Cruz is on top of things, Syn thought, *if that's his name. The signature is about as legible as any other doctor's. Do they teach bad penmanship in medical school? Shame he didn't think about it until the third body fell. Ah well, at least he thought about it.*

Finally, Syn studied the crime scene photos. Copies of the photos really. 4x5 contact prints from the negatives. Overall shots to establish the scene and show approaches, some mid-range of the victims, close-ups of their faces and wounds. Syn wished for more but the crime scene guy could only carry so many photographic plates.

Syn was done. He had a secondhand sense of what the scenes were like. In the morning before going into the office, he'd visit the crime scenes and maybe pay a call on Dr. Delacruz, ask him some questions, and maybe tell him a thing or two he won't believe.

Looking at the clock, Syn wondered if it was too late to wake his wife up for that kiss. If not, he hoped Jericho was asleep. Cara could get kinda loud sometimes.

Chapter Four

The pack's crossing of what humans called Chincoteague Bay was uneventful, other than convincing the younger cubs to enter the water. While swimming came naturally to the pack, its members usually avoided deep water, so the cubs were fearful. Two of the youths solved the problem by mouthing the necks of the reluctant cubs and throwing them in as Revna and the other adults watched with amusement, approval, and no concerns for their safety. Best that those who would not or could not swim leave the pack now. Fortunately, all survived their sudden immersion, but the adults noted the hesitant ones. Weakness could only harm the pack.

We will need food, thought Dagr to Revna once the crossing was made and they were on unfamiliar ground. He had been Revna's mate in the last season and so thought himself in a position to give the new pack leader unneeded advice.

She considered snarling at him but decided that it had not been a challenge.

Reilly told me that there will be what humans call farms along the way. On these farms humans raise beasts for milk and food. He advised that we hunt carefully and not disturb them.

And what of the humans themselves? Embla asked. She was the oldest and, as such, rich in wisdom and pack lure. She might have been chosen as leader had she not made it clear she did not want to lead.

The ones that came to shore some seasons past were lean and tasty, Revna sent back with a pause. *But not as tasty as other beasts. Still, should the pack come across one or two walking alone at night…*

Traveling by night and hiding during the day, Revna's pack crossed from one small body of water to a larger one in two days. On the first night, they took down a deer. The frightened beast ran fast but with the cubs following, the youths gave chase and herded it toward the adults. Idunn made the kill and so, along with Revna, ate first. The remaining adults ate next, followed by the youths and cubs. One of the youths, Taoke, tried to push forward past the adults. He was cuffed for this effort and made to wait until all the others had eaten, but some of the adults noted his daring.

They continued west, hiding and sleeping by day, traveling and hunting by night. They fed on deer, cows, goats, whatever they came across. Soon they were close to the great water. One more sleep before they crossed to "home," a place they had never been before. It was near daylight when they returned to the rough den they had made in the woods when they caught the mixed scent of man and horse.

Like the dway, Trace Norton traveled from one end of the peninsula to the other. He had left Captains Cove some days ago in no hurry to return to his Crisfield home, taking time to visit friends along the way. Now, close enough that he imagined he could smell the breakfast that his aunt Louise would cook him on his arrival, he had decided to travel by night so he could arrive in time for that meal. Both he and his horse Barney knew the way through the woods so he was not expecting trouble.

Instead, he heard growling behind him. His senses more acute, Barney smelled the creatures coming up fast behind him. He did not recognize their scent but knew it was not a friendly one. When his rider cracked the reins and urged him to a gallop, the horse did not hesitate. Too bad for man and horse that the dway hunted in packs.

Dagr jumped from a tree, knocking Norton from his saddle. The human's blood tasted sweet as it gushed from his throat. Dagr was quickly joined by some of the youths and cubs.

The rest of the pack ran down the horse. Barney kicked out, striking one of them but was no match for the rest. Revna ripped his throat and drank his blood then joined the rest of the pack in feasting on his body.

The pack ate its fill and then some, gathering strength for the next night's long swim. Only Powr did not eat. It was Taoke who found him, lying where the horse had kicked him. Taoke sent to Revna who came quickly.

Powr has left the pack, she thought to the others. With four youths carrying Powr's body, they abandoned their temporary den and went deep into the woods to sleep for the day. The man and horse were left where they fell.

Daylight came, the adults taking turns sleeping and guarding. There were distant noises from the humans who found the remains of the horse and its rider. When Dagr and the youth Etok heard the humans draw closer, they prepared to wake the pack to either flee or fight. But the voices faded again.

When Dagr woke Revna, he told her what he heard. Together they sniffed the air. There were faint traces of human scent on the morning breeze but too far away to worry about. *You and Etok sleep*, Revna sent to Dagr. *Inkir and I will watch and wake the pack when it is time.*

The light faded and gave way to the dark. The pack roused and fed on what they had carried away from the previous night's kill. The food was not fresh but it was filling.

As one they stood on the eastern shore of the great water. Revna was about to order them in when she felt a presence. It was not human, but it was not of the pack.

Wait, she sent. And as she did so, a great serpent emerged from the water at a distance from the shore. Up and up it rose, until the part of it that was showing was three times the height of the tallest dwayyo.

You seek to enter my waters, it thought to Revna.

And you are? The pack leader answered in challenge.

There was a tone of amusement in the creature's reply. *I am C'cil, called Chessie by men. I guard this bay and protect those who live and swim in it. Most of those at least. Will you be crossing and why?*

Revna sensed no threat in C'cil's words, just wondering. *We cross in search of a new den.*

Yours on the island of ponies has grown too large then.

You knew of the pack?

I know much about the waters and those who live in or around them. Just as I know that if you would cross, you'd best do it quickly. Men come. Men with weapons. Men full of anger.

The dway were so intent on the crossing they had failed to detect the humans. Now they did. Revna would have ordered the pack to turn and face this threat but C'cil stopped her.

Do not fight them. They are hunting those who killed one of their own, as is their right.

We are on land. How will you stop us from the water?

I cannot not. I will not. But those of you who survive the fight with the men will find their passage across my bay a dangerous one. Those who make it to the western shore may not be enough to form a pack.

Revna considered the words of the great serpent. Without acknowledging the threat, she sent instructions to the pack.

Youths, go and help the cubs. Dagr, Egil, Embla, guard against the humans.

The pack then entered the waters of the bay. They were quick but so were the men. Spurred on by the dogs used to track them, who sensed in the dway a territorial threat, the men were coming closer.

Have we time? sent Embla. The three guards knew it was a matter of minutes before the humans came out of the woods and on to the beach.

The pack does, Dagr replied. *But as for us, I do not know.*

Embla did not hesitate. *Then go,* she sent to Dagr and Egil. *Remember me.* And she ran toward the scent of the humans and dogs.

A quarter of the pack was still on shore when Dagr and Egil returned.

Where is Embla? asked Revna.

Doing what she must for the pack, came Egil's reply.

Revna nodded in understanding then watched her pack leave the shore. With one last look toward the woods, she entered the bay.

One last thing, C'cil sent to Revna, *there is a storm coming. It may fall over the bay before you make it to land. I would advise you to wait but...*

Growls, snarls, barks, screams, and gunshots came from the woods.

...I do not think waiting would be wise.

The dwayyo swan off. C'cil waited until they were some distance away. Then noises from the shore attracted her attention.

"There they are," shouted Fred Cox. He had been in the lead, just behind the dogs. From where he stood, he could see the shore and the monsters who stood on it. They were things out of a nightmare, and he was both scared and amazed at their size. Then he looked out on the bay. There he saw what he had thought was only legend.

"It's Chessie," he shouted to the other men. "And she's holding the monsters off for us."

The men would have fired from the safety of the woods but just then something large with dark grey fur, sharp claws, and sharper teeth moved among them. One or two of the men ran and would forever be ashamed of doing so, even considering how things turned out. The others shook off their fear and fired on the monster in their midst, trying not to hit the dogs who had already joined in the attack.

As she ran among the trees, Embla sent thoughts of fear and surrender toward her prey. It worked on some of the dogs and humans but the rest were too enraged to be affected. The dogs came at her first, jumping at her, biting, tearing. As Embla fought them off, the men fired their guns. Time and again bullets and pellets struck and entered her body, though some hit the dogs. Shaking off most of the dogs, carrying the rest with her, growling in challenge and defiance, Embla lunged amidst the men, doing her own biting and tearing. Two of the men, Fred Cox and Jimmy Schultz, managed to withdraw.

"Headshots?" asked Jimmy.

"Headshots," Fred agreed.

"We might hit the others."

"Too late for them anyway."

Both men fired. Jimmy's first shot grazed Embla's head. Fred's shot missed its intended target but took the beast square in the chest.

Embla shook off her now mostly dead attacker and charged toward the new threat. Jimmy and Fred got off two more shots before taking the better part of valor. They turned to run.

Embla stumbled but caught herself. She had taken too many wounds and knew she would soon leave the pack. But she still needed to protect her kind. Reaching the two, her claws ripped Jimmy's back open then snapped Fred's neck.

Alone among the moaning and whimpering, Embla turned toward the shore. Her pack was safe, she had saved them. Her spirit satisfied, she walked slowly into the water. With no hope of catching up with the others, her only goal was to swim out far enough so that her body would not be found.

C'cil had watched and listened to the battle on the land, sensed each death as it occurred. As she thought, *This will come to no good*, she saw a lone figure walking toward the shore. It was the one called Embla.

C'cil felt the dway's intention, to lose herself in the water. When the dway died not far from shore, C'cil took her body in her jaws and carried it far into the bay. Then she followed the remaining dwayyo both out of curiosity and concern for the creatures who were in her waters and under her protection.

When I next see the Scarecrow, she thought, *I will have to tell him of this.*

It was a one-night swim. The pack was an hour away from the western shore of the bay when the storm C'cil had warned it about struck. The winds came in hard and the waves were large and rough. The dwayyo, who up until then had kept close together, were buffeted and scattered. Etok was lost, all the dway felt him slip beneath the water and leave the pack. The hour left to swim turned into two, then three. There was but an hour left of darkness when most of the pack washed up on the shore. Mental links were quickly established and most of the pack gathered.

I do not feel Fiske, or Bjar, or Taoke, thought Dagr to the pack.

Bjar is gone, Egil sent. *I felt him leave the pack.*

And there is Fiske. Aslg indicated an unmoving figure that still lay on the beach. As the pack moved toward her, they felt her leave the pack.

That left Taoke. No one in the pack had felt the youth leave so, using their minds, they searched for a trace of him. They found none.

Daylight comes, warned Revna. *Let us find a safe place to sleep. Tomorrow night we will hunt, feed, and search for Taoke as we make our way to the mountain that is to be our home. Or perhaps he will find us.*

Guided by instinct and Reilly's instructions, the pack made its way, traveling by night, hunting and killing what game they found. Having learned how dangerous humans could be the pack avoided all contact with them. Despite keeping their minds open for his call, none of the dwayyo sensed or felt Taoke. He has left the pack, they collectively decided.

The pack made it to Corbet Woods without incident. Before they settled their new den, Revna sent out the adults, each accompanied by a youth, to scout the area. No dangers were found. The flying ones were asleep atop the mountain. This area would be avoided unless the flying ones woke up. And the pack was deep enough in the woods that contact with humans would be rare. Should one or two wander close to the den, too bad for them. This far in, what was left of their bodies would not be found.

Two weeks after the dway established their den, Patricia Joseph was brutally murdered.

Chapter Five

When the winds came up and the waves stuck, Taoke went under. When he emerged from the blackness of the water, he had turned around and swam off at an angle. Frightened, alone in the dark, he did not think to reach out to his pack. Instead, he swam to catch up to them, each stroke taking him farther and farther away. He was still swimming when the pack made shore. By this time, he was too confused to sense their sendings. So, he swam, swam until he could swim no more. His limbs ached, his mind drifted, his will failed. He stopped, gave himself to the waters of the bay, and sank beneath the surface.

He would have drowned, his body becoming food for the creatures of the bay, but C'cil had been following the pack. During the storm, she had gently nudged one or two of the dway that had fallen back. Some she could not save, being busy with others. From a distance, she watched as the pack staggered to land. Her job done, she swam away, thinking to swim the underocean for a time. But then she felt a mind in distress. She swam to it and arrived in time to see a dway being taken by the water. Sensing that life remained, she nudged it first to the surface then toward land, watched as the youth slowly drifted to the shore, then swam away.

On the morning following the rains, Orville and Wilbur Smith, twelve-year-old twins whose unfortunate names were the result of their mother's passion for aviation, walked the shoreline along the east coast of the Chesapeake Bay. They did this every morning after a heavy storm, hoping to find that something interesting or valuable had been washed up. Once they found an oak chest full of books. The books were too sodden to read but the junk man in Reedville (he called himself an antiques dealer but no one else did) paid them five dollars for it. This time, however, they found something quite different.

At first Orv and Will, as everyone but their mother called them, thought it a dead body, drowned by the storm. However, once they ran up to it, they discovered that not only did it seem alive, but it did not appear human. It was about five feet, covered in fur, heavily built, naked and obviously male.

"Looks like a wolf," Orv said.

"Don't look like no wolf I ever seen," Will replied.

"You ever see a wolf?"

"Once, in a circus."

Will's mention of the circus got both boys thinking. "Ain't there a circus in town?" he asked his brother.

Orv ran to get his father. Will watched their find from a distance, hoping that it would not wake up and prepared to defend it should someone else come along.

No one else came long and Taoke did not wake up, not until he had been bound in heavy chains and on his way as the new star attraction of The Stone Brothers Traveling Circus, Carnival, and Natural Odditys Exhibition.

Chapter Six

"I thought Detective Lynch was in charge of this investigation?" Dr. Dela Cruz asked.

"He is," admitted Syn, trying not to show the surprise he felt when he first met the doctor.

"So why are you asking about the victims of the Beast?" Dr. Cruz laughed at her own question. Her laugh was enhanced by an accent that Syn had yet to place. "Sounds like a cheaply made horror film, doesn't it?"

Syn smiled. It was easy to smile at Dela Cruz. She was a tall, full-figured woman with dark hair and eyes with a skin tone that suggested some place south of Texas. Yet there was something more than Mexico in that laugh.

"Life's like that sometimes," he said, knowing that scary monsters weren't just on the movie screen. "I'm following another line of inquiry."

Cruz and Syn were in her office on the first floor of the Harbor City Medical Examiner's Office. Below them were the morgue and examination room. Dr. Cruz was the pathologist who performed the autopsy on Patricia Joseph. As a result, the other victims of what was being called "the Beast" fell under, as she put it, "her concern."

"Another line of inquiry?" she said, as much to herself as to Syn. "Is that police talk for they sent the Scarecrow to see if the Beast really was a monster rather than a monstrous human? Oh, don't look so surprised. My grandfather was part of the Burke gang during the Roadhouse Wars. When the *mierda* broke loose and people started getting killed or arrested, *mi Abuelo* took his family and headed south. He didn't stop until he crossed the Rio Grande. That's where he met my mother and where I was born."

"So why come back to Harbor City?" Syn suspected he knew that answer, but married life had taught him never to assume anything about what a woman thought.

Another laugh. *I could get lost in that laugh*, Syn thought. "For the monsters, of course. From what *mi Abuelo* told me, there used to be a lot of them. And from what he and others have said, you knew some of those monsters and have the marks to prove it."

Syn kept an even expression, neither confirming nor denying Cruz's implied question. "Dr. Cruz..."

"Please, call me Dela. And can I call you... what, Theodore, Ted, Scarecrow?"

Syn shrugged. "Doesn't matter. Now about the three victims..."

"You know, Scarecrow, on a professional level I would love to exam those marks you're supposed to have. She took a deep breath and a chance. "I wouldn't mind on a personal level either."

Syn was surprised. It wasn't often that he was propositioned so boldly. He thought that Dela Cruz either liked tall, slender men with uncombed hair or the idea of monsters really excited her. To answer Cruz, Syn held up his left hand, allowing light from the window to reflect off his wedding ring.

There was a little more Dublin than Mexico City in Cruz's voice when she said, "Damn. It seems that the only men I get to meet are married, dead, or doctors. And the last are the worst. They tend to see me as a nurse who can do tricks, sort of like a trained dog. Or, as Doctor Charles Lethem put it, 'Nothing but a smart bitch.' Now then, about those women." Dr. Cruz shifted into professional mode. "One of them is still here. Her body has been released but the funeral home hasn't picked her up yet. Would you like to see her?"

Syn said he would, and Cruz took him downstairs to the autopsy room. With his help, Cruz got the cloth-wrapped body of Rosie Donovan on the table. Cruz then opened the sheet covering Donovan's body for Syn's examination.

Syn had seen death many times. including the victims of both the snallygaster and the dwayyo. Rosie Donovan's body was not as bad as they were. Still, every violent death saddened him. In his mind, the deceased called out for justice. Maybe that's why he did what he did. He never really thought about it too much, except in cases like this when the call was more of a scream for vengeance.

Syn looked over the dead woman. Her wounds and condition were as they were described in the autopsy reports. "The missing organs, did you remove them or did the killer?"

"You read the report. Some were removed by the killer, the rest by me."

Syn nodded. "And were there any signs that any part of Miss Donovan was consumed?"

"Again," a now somewhat irritated Cruz replied, "it would have been in the report."

"Unless the report was altered. Monsters eating people is not good for the city's image."

"I don't think the devil himself could hurt Harbor City's image. But no, no part of any of the victims appeared to have been eaten."

"No monster then." Syn grabbed one end of the sheet and began covering Rosie Donovan up. "At least, not the ones I've encountered. They would have eaten some if not most of the victims. Some would have sucked their blood right through their skin." He then helped her place the body in its temporary stainless-steel crypt to await pick up. The two washed up and Cruz escorted Syn upstairs.

"Thank you, Dela. Should a body like the rest come under your care, please call me." He gave her his office and home numbers.

"And if your wife answers?"

"Just tell her you have a body for me to look at." To which a small part of his mind commented, *And she does.* But he thought of Cara and the thought went away.

"When I told Dr. Cruz that no monster was involved, I wasn't telling the whole truth," Syn told Jack Fuller when he made his report.

"You mean there really is a monster?" the lieutenant asked.

Syn shook his head. "Just the human kind, one I wouldn't mind introducing to some of the creatures I've met. But the only one still around is Chessie, and she doesn't like how we taste. No, Jack, this one belongs to Lynch."

Chapter Seven

I write as Chastel. It is an old family name; one whose blood is over three hundred years old. We have been heroes and monsters, doing what we must to survive and protect the family.

Long ago, in France, we hunted the beasts and were hunted by them. We killed them and they killed us until both sides were almost extinct. Then Antoine Chastel and his wife Jeanne were attacked by a pack in season. What happened then was known but never talked about, never written down. Suffice to say that they survived, and the curse was passed on down both lines, ours and theirs, or so goes the legend.

Soon after, there were many deaths in the region of Gevaudan. The peasants complained and the king's government, for once, became involved. Sacrifices were made. Etienne Chastel took blame for some deaths and the wolves for others. The army and royal huntsmen were satisfied.

Then came the mad times. Some of the family joined La Revolution. Some met the sharp kiss of Lady Guillotine. The rest fled. Our cousins, the wolves grew fat. They owned the countryside and even dared the streets of Paris. At times, the Chastels ran with them. All did what was needed to survive. With some much death and blood, no one questioned the source the bodies.

Napoleon came. One terror ended and another began. Both family and pack were hunted for their crimes, killed, forgotten except for stories and legends.

What happened to the pack is not known. The family dispersed—Paris, Madrid, London, overseas to the Americas. But the curse of Antoine and Jeanne's sins followed and remained in the blood. We did not, as some supposed, become beasts nor did we fear the Moon. But sometimes the madness rose in us.

It is strong, this madness. I know, for it is in me. As a teen I felt it, dreamed it. Nightmares of terror and murder. I would wake up hot and sweaty and pleasure myself to the memory of those dreams even as I longed to return to them. But it was not until I received a set of sharp-edged gauntlets — a legacy from a grand-mere I had never known — that I recognized the curse for what it was. Wearing them for a few moments before sleep, thinking of how they might be used, how they had been used, sweetened the dreams, and increased the pleasure of what I did upon waking.

And that was enough. For a time. A long time. I was an adult, respected, with a good job. A profession. A more or less normal life. But still, at least once a week, the gauntlets then sleep, then dreams, then pleasure. Then the dreams became chaotic, less distinct, more longing than doing. No pleasure when I woke no matter how much I…

The dreams were not enough. I put on the knife-edged gauntlets and hunted the night.

The first was a woman reading on a bench. There was an air about her, of anger and elation. Of strength and weakness. She had fought and had both won and lost. I did not care about this, just that she was alone and vulnerable. I gave into the Beast. I became the Beast. Took my pleasure in the moment. That night I slept deeply and woke satisfied.

The second was almost at her door, feeling safe and satisfied about suppressed urges. There was another. I was hoping he'd move to protect his desired mate, but he stank of fear and let me kill her.

I had watched the third for some time. Watched her satisfying men. When she was done with the last one, I followed until she was alone. When I attacked her, she accepted it and I sensed some relief that, for her, it was all over.

But not for me. Once the dreams begin to lose their vividness, once the pleasure on waking is no longer as intense, I will hunt again.

Chapter Eight

A week went by with no progress on the Beast case. On the bright side, there were no new murders like those of Rosie Donovan and the others. No one in Homicide took much comfort in that. They all knew that this kind of killer didn't stop, merely falling dormant until he felt the urge to kill again.

Detective Lynch did everything he could. He looked for connections in the lives of the victims—their hobbies, their boyfriends (in Rosie's case her clients), where they lived, where they used to live, the schools they went to. No connections except how they died.

Detective Ritchie suggested putting out bait, looking at Jane Higgins as he said it.

"I'm not his type," Higgins said. She knew the killer liked them young and pretty and she didn't see herself as either. She would have been surprised that several members of the squad thought of her as both. "But if you think it will help..."

"No," Lynch interrupted her offer. "My case. I'll dress up and do it. Alone, in the dark, the killer might go for it."

"If you do, Adam, I'll be there for you," Syn offered. He didn't like Lynch much but he respected a brave man. "I'll make sure you won't be hurt too badly. At worst he won't get away." Syn said this without a smile. He wasn't joking, just laying out the stakes.

"Enough of that," Lieutenant Fuller snapped. "No one's playing Judas goat and if Chief Stockbridge asks us to, I'll ask him how he looks in a dress. Meanwhile, Lynch, keep working the case. The weapon used was an odd one. Try checking museums as well as weapon experts and collectors to try to identify it. Let me know what help you need, and I'll see that you get it. And all of you, let's get ready if and when there's a fourth killing. If there is, let's pray that this guy makes a mistake, or someone gets a good look at him. In the meantime…"

Fuller handed Syn a piece of paper with an address. "Head out to the fairgrounds. There's some kind of circus set up. Some clown's gotten himself killed."

When Syn arrived at the Harbor City Fairgrounds, he was surprised to see most of the circus was in full operation. Customers were going in and out of the main tent. The carnival rides and games were operating. Looking to the right of where the concourse was set up, he saw patrol cars and a roped-off area in front of a tent with a sign that read "Oddi-tys of the World." He noted idly that "Oddities" was misspelled but figured the sign painter had run out of room.

"Detective Syn. What do we have, Brady?" Syn asked reading the cop's name tag.

"In here, detective." Brady started to lead him into the tent. Syn held him up.

"Why weren't the rides, games, and show shut down?"

Brady shook his head. "It was all running by the time we got here. The Sarge said the damage was done and to let them go. At least the body's still here. Usually, when something happens, they take the body out to the road to be found. This time it's a special case."

"Where is your sergeant?"

"You'll find him inside, in the 'men only' section, guarding the 'Exotic Women of the World.' But don't worry. Henderson's watching the body. It's in the back."

"Odditys of the World" was, as Syn had expected from its name, the circus's freak show. Syn didn't like either the name or the show itself. But, he reasoned, "freaks" is how the performers referred to themselves and shows like this were the only way most of them could make a living.

The exhibit was a carefully laid out labyrinth, designed to lead customers through it without giving them the chance to double back. To see something again they'd have to pay another admission. Leaving Brady on guard, Syn entered, trusting that somewhere on the winding path he'd find Officer Henderson and a sheet-covered body.

Along the way, he passed very short people, an extremely tall man, a very heavy bearded lady, a fire eater, a rubber man, a snake woman, and Jacky the half-a-man. With no customers present, all of them relaxed in some way or another.

At the first turn, Syn came to a large tank of water next to which sat a woman clad in a not-too-revealing seashell bra and a fish tail. The sign above her space proclaimed her "Pacifica, the Galapagos Mermaid." Syn was sure that inside her tank she was quite convincing but out of it, it was quite clear her tail was made of rubber. Syn must have lingered a bit too long because she looked at him and, in a Bronx accent, said, "It's further on, two turns and you'll find it."

"Forgive Miss, eh, Pacifica, but with no customers present, why don't you take off your tail and relax? I mean, it must be hot."

"It's damned hot, copper, but it's a bitch to take off and put on and they tell me that once you guys leave the show can open. Besides, I'm not wearing any panties and my legs only go down to my knees. That's why I got into this mermaid gig. And since you're homicide and not vice, I'll tell you for nothing that some guys dig what I haven't got, if you know what I mean."

Syn knew. He nodded a farewell and moved on.

"Wait," Pacifica called out, "take a card. They cost a buck but what the hell."

Syn turned back and picked one up. He had noticed that all the performers had cards and pamphlets for sale. Pacifica's showed her in her tank, her seashell bra hanging on the edge. The water was just cloudy enough to suggest nudity without revealing it.

"Worth a buck," Syn said politely and, because he was an honest cop, fished a dollar from his wallet and left it for her.

"Thanks," she said. "That gets you a special one." With a well-practiced flip, Pacifica sent another card flying toward him. On this one the water was clear. With a "Thanks," Syn slipped both cards into his inside jacket pocket and moved on.

Two turns later he came to the main crime scene. Officer Henderson stood close to the sheet-wrapped victim. There were three others present. One introduced himself as Evan Stone, manager and part owner of the circus. The other two were a fish-faced man and one with hair that covered most of his face but for his slightly slanted eyes who introduced himself as "Shiu, the Monkey Prince." He was dressed in a modified harem guard's outfit, cut to display his extremely hirsute legs and chest. As he greeted Syn he said, "Actually my father was a grocer in Kansas City, but no one wants to see Henry the grocer's son."

The thing to do, the thing Syn wanted to do, had to do, was to lift the sheet and look at the body. But that sort of thing was best done without civilians present. So, before he sent them away, he asked, "Who found the body?"

"Actually, he found us, me and Henry," said the fishman, whose real name was Nick but who performed under the name Nemo of the Deep. "We were just getting set up for the first of the looky-loos when he came through the back flap, staggered a bit, and fell in front of us."

"You know him then?"

"Yeah, we do," answered Stone for all three men. Letting out a sigh of sorrow, the manager said, "It's Franklin Hays. He's one of our whiteface clowns. Performs… *performed* under the name Frodo, said he got the name from a book."

"As I remember, Boss," Henry said with a half-hearted grin, "It used to be Bilbo only we kept… mispronouncing it, so he changed to Frodo."

"Yeah, right. Anyway, Detective Syn, I may as well be the one to tell you 'cause everyone knows, we kind of know who the killer is."

"Oh?" *It can't be that easy*, Syn thought. *They never are.*

"Last night Frank here walked into his trailer a bit early and caught his wife Amy, she works the carnival fishpond by day and dances at the late-night show, in bed with our knife thrower Ricardo. His real name's Kevin Black but he goes by Ricardo all the time. There were words, and threats, and some punches thrown. Frank beat up Ricardo pretty bad. After he threw him out of the trailer, I think there were more punches thrown."

"And where are Amy and this Ricardo now?"

Stone shook his head. "Can't find them, and trust me on this, we searched this place better than you cops could."

Just then there came a muffled bestial roar, one that took Syn back to the Roadhouse War when it was gangster versus gangster, and man against beast. The men lost. The snallygasters withdrew to the mountains, and the dwayyo to the Eastern Shore. Another roar and it was all Syn could do not to run toward it.

"Just our new exhibit," Stone explained. "Grimm, the Big Bad Wolf. It's off in a side tent, extra admission required, like with our exotic beauties."

"Which reminds me," Syn said, turning to Henderson, "You've gotten statements from these three men, right?" The officer nodded.

"Good. I'll watch things here. You find your sergeant and tell him to take statements from the rest of the, um…"

"You can say freaks, detective," the Monkey Prince said, "that's what we are."

"The rest of the performers," Syn went on.

"But they didn't see anything."

"Which we have to make sure of. Tell him brief statements along with real and stage names, and he's to pay for any cards he takes, including the ones of the exotic beauties. If I find out otherwise, he'll be on nighttime foot patrol in the Wild Western."

Henderson went off. Addressing the others, Syn said, "Gentlemen, I am sorry for your loss but now you'll have to excuse me while I examine Mr. Hays's body."

"Uh, Detective Syn, so you mind if we stay just a bit after you uncover him?" asked Stone. "Just for a minute, to say good-bye."

Syn allowed that they could and knelt to uncover the victim. When he did, he found that Fuller wasn't joking when he said some clown got killed. Under the sheet was a whiteface clown with a round, red nose and spiky hair. He wore a red and blue costume with white buttons. Syn expected big, red shoes but instead the clown was barefoot.

When the three circus people gathered around him to pay their last respects Henry said, "Something's wrong."

"Yeah," agreed Nick. "But I just can't place what it is."

Maybe it's because he's dead, Syn thought but then Stone asked,

"Can you wipe off the makeup?"

"Not yet," Syn replied, but he suddenly had a feeling about what they would find.

Henderson came back. "I told the Sarge, detective. And he had more than a few choice words about you, your family, and what you all do in your spare time."

"He's welcome to his opinion. Now find a phone, get enough men here to keep people in and out."

"Trouble?"

"Maybe. Right now, it's just a feeling."

Far ahead of them, the Big Bad Wolf growled again.

Chapter Nine

The crime scene people arrived. They photographed the dead clown, the entrances and exits, the way to the Hays' trailer, and inside the trailer. Syn was there for the last. If there had been a fight, all signs of it had been cleaned up. The crime lab techs searched for blood, weapons, and latent prints. They found many of the latter, but comparison would have to wait until they got back to the lab.

The Medical Examiner arrived just after the crime lab was done. It was Doctor Lethem, who several times expressed his displeasure at being called away from his work to, as he put it, "Take a look at some dead, damned freak."

"You got it wrong, Doc," Henry the Monkey Prince corrected. "He's a clown. We're the freaks." Lethem ignored him and directed his people to take photos. "Don't see why you needed a pathologist for this," he all but snarled at Syn.

"Just being thorough, doctor," the detective answered. Was that it, Syn wondered, or was he hoping that Dela Cruz would be the one who responded? "I need to wipe the makeup off the deceased face and wanted you to see it as it was first."

"You can't do that here. That's done at the…"

Despite his sometimes-comical appearance, the Scarecrow could be quite intimidating when he wanted to be. His "I wasn't asking, doctor," was close to threatening and caused Lethem to shut up and back off.

At Syn's direction, Officer Brady, who had been relieved of guard duty by Officer Henderson, wiped the face of the victim clean. He was only half done when Evan Stone shouted,

"Hell, that's not Frank! That's, that's, damn it, it's Ricardo."

And here I thought this was going to be easy, Syn thought. *Or maybe, it just got easier*. It was Stone who said what Syn had almost immediately figured out.

"Frank killed him for messing with Amy then put him in his own costume to buy himself some time. That's why he left the shoes off. Ricardo had bigger feet."

"Maybe that's why Amy took up with him," Nick said. No one laughed.

"Then he's probably long gone," Brady suggested.

"Maybe not," Syn said. "His job might only be half-finished. Mr. Stone, you said your people searched everywhere on the grounds?"

"Yeah, but they were looking for Ricardo, not Frank."

It was cruel to ask, but Syn had to. "And Amy? Were they searching for her, or her body?" The look on Stone's face gave him the answer.

By then extra officers had arrived, along with the current Police Academy class. "Okay, Mr. Stone, the whole place gets searched again, one of your people teamed with one of ours. If you see Frank or Amy cry out."

"Will do, Detective Syn. If you hear, 'Hey, rube!' you come a running."

The search began. As Syn waited with Brady as the ME team prepared the body of Kevin Black for transport, he asked himself where Amy Hays might be, assuming she was hiding and not hidden. Both she and her husband knew the grounds. Where could she hide that he couldn't find her?

Where do you hide a book? he asked himself. *Or a tree?* Syn got a hunch on where Amy might be. *If I'm wrong, I'm wrong, but there's definitely no harm in looking.*

He headed for The Exotic World of Women.

There were two separate tents joined to the Sideshow tent. The poster on the first one read "Come see the Big Bad Wolf!" The wolf on the poster stood on two legs, his claws reaching out to menace a red-caped beauty. The wolf was disturbingly familiar. He dismissed this as artistic license, but he'd check later just to make sure.

Syn moved toward the second tent. The poster there showed a number of good-looking women scantily dressed in what were supposed to be their native costumes. He was about to go in when,

Scarecrow.

The thought was loud in his mind and had come from outside it. Without hesitation, he turned and went in to see the Big, Bad Wolf.

There was a cage. In it was a dwayyo, standing behind heavy, iron bars. By the size of him, he was a youth, but even a young dwayyo stood as tall as a man and had the advantage of reach and weight.

Scarecrow, Syn heard again.

You know me?

Your story has been told. There was no menace, no hatred in the sending. Maybe a little respect. *You seek a male and female?*

I do.

The female is close, among other females. No pictures were sent but there was no doubt that the dway meant the tent next to his. *The male waits. He has taken one from our pack. He wants to take another, the female, his mate.* There was disgust in the dway's thoughts, disgust that one member of the pack (*Did he say,* our *pack?* Syn thought.) and more disgust that he would seek to kill his mate.

Where does he wait?

This time the dway linked his mind to Syn's, showing the detective exactly where Franklin Hays was.

Thank you, Syn sent. *We will talk again.*

Syn turned to leave the tent and almost bumped into a thin, small cop with sergeant stripes on his sleeve.

"Hey, Detective Syn," he said in a nervous, high-pitched voice, "what the hell…?" Syn stepped aside, giving Sergeant Barnabas a clear view of the dway. "Jesus H. Christ!" Instinctively the sergeant reached for his revolver.

"Don't!" Syn ordered in a commanding voice. "He's a friend of mine. Now follow me, sergeant, we have a killer to catch."

Syn picked up Brady on the way as well as Henderson. He led them to the parking area where the trucks and other equipment not used for the circus itself were parked. There stood a worker clad in circus coveralls. He crouched behind a pickup truck.

The cops saw him before he saw them. At Syn's cry of "Frodo!" he turned and thought to run. But Barnabas had worked around him. The sergeant stood in a firing stance, pointing his revolver at Hays in a two-handed grip.

"Drop the knife," Barnabas said in his reedy voice.

Three cops on one side of him. One cop on the other side taking deadly aim. Hays hesitated. He almost dropped the knife. But instead, he rushed Barnabas.

Maybe he thought he could get past the sergeant. Maybe Hays thought he would miss. Maybe he knew full well what would happen and decided not to go to jail.

Sergeant Andrew Barnabas fired once, and Franklin Hays collapsed in a lifeless heap.

After relieving him of his service weapon, Officer Brady led his shaken sergeant away.

"Guess that Dr. Lethem will be pissed at having to come back here," Henderson said to Syn.

Or maybe, Syn thought guiltily, *Dr. Cruz will come out.* "Stand by the body, Henderson. I'll have someone come and relieve you soon. I have to tell Mr. Stone that he should be able to open the tent for the evening show and then I have someone to talk to."

When evening fell, the carnival's lights came on, letting Harbor City know that the show would go on.

It was a larger crowd than usual, spurred on by news and rumors of what had happened. Some heard that a lion had gotten loose, others that the Big Bad Wolf had escaped. Murder on a mass scale was reported, involving clowns, carnies, and exotic dancers. From the ring master to the animal shoveler, all the circus folk were told, if asked, to deny everything but in a way that suggested that it might be true. Of course, none of them had to be told since they all knew not to let the truth get in the way of a good story.

Dr. Cruz responded to the scene. A police officer-involved shooting required the presence of a pathologist. If she were hoping to see Theodore Syn, she was disappointed. He was, she was told, busy elsewhere. That did not stop her from looking for him and asking questions.

Inside the oddities tent, all of the performers save one were ready to display themselves, to face the public, and to sell their photos and pamphlets. One of the special tents remained closed. A sign outside it read "Sorry, the Big Bad Wolf is visiting Grandma tonight. He will be back tomorrow." One or two people asked for a refund only to be told that since admission to see the wolf was extra, they would not be getting their quarter back.

Theodore Syn had been in the Big Bad Wolf's tent most of the day, ever since he told Evan Stone that his circus could reopen. He and the young dwayyo had "talked" most of that time.

Syn entered the tent carrying a folding chair. When he opened it and sat down, the dway came close to the bars of its cage and sat on its haunches.

The detective introduced himself. *I am Theodore Syn.*

That is what you are called, you are *the Scarecrow,* replied the dway, echoing something a sea creature had once told the detective. *I am Taoke.*

When Syn asked, *How did you come here?* Taoke told him of the splitting of the pack, the journeys across land and water, and the storm. He did not hold back the dway's killing of the deer, the horse and rider, or the battle with the men. To Taoke, these were not something to conceal.

Where is the rest of your pack?

Syn's question confused Taoke. *This is my pack. I lost my old one in the storm. The stone people found me, saved me, fed me. They are now my pack.*

Even though they cage you?

Taoke's mouth opened, showing long, sharp teeth. From his mouth came "Huh, huh, huh" — dwayyo laughter. The dway stood, shook the bars of the cage door, and sat again.

I cage myself. If I wanted, I believe that I could break this door. But I have not tried. I have not tried to reach my old pack, whom I sense in the distance. They would come to save me and there would be much blood and food. And that would hurt my pack that is. And should my pack that was come and kill and feed, the humans would hunt us. And even though they have abandoned me, I cannot hurt my pack that was. And I will not hurt my pack that is. So, I remain by choice.

How do you know me? Syn asked.

The human called Reilly told the larger pack of you and others. He said that you fought and killed members of the pack. I would know more.

Again, Syn did not sense any menace or hatred in the mind of the young dway. He took a chance.

By a bond of blood, I was accepted into a flock of the snallygaster, what you call the flying ones. In the last battle between your pack and my flock, I stayed to protect my flock's young. To do so I had to kill two of your pack.

They left the pack while fighting?

Yes, and were eaten by their enemy.

A part of them is then a part of the flying ones. This is good. Thank you, Scarecrow. Tell me more of your kind and I will tell you of mine.

Syn and Taoke sat and opened their minds. Neither quite understood the other but there was peace in their sharing. Soon they were done.

It is late. And time for me to go to my sleeping den. Soon daylight comes and I will work for the good of the pack.

Why do you do it, Taoke, when you could easily leave?

I serve my pack, Scarecrow, and... there was that "Huh, huh, huh" again *...I like scaring the marks. Their fear feeds me in a way prey once did.*

This last sent a shudder of concern through Syn. He had to ask.

Taoke, have you ever left your den and gone outside the pack home?

Why would I, Scarecrow?

Syn tried not to think of three young women who had been ripped apart. *No reason, Taoke. Sleep well.*

Syn left Taoke and went to see Evan Stone.

"Everything good?" the manager asked.

"Everything's good, so far. The Big Bad Wolf, you know he's smarter than the average wolf?"

"Yeah, I had a sense. I think some of the others do too. I also get a sense that he's, well, not as dangerous as he looks."

"He's more dangerous than you can imagine, Mr. Stone. But treat him right and he'll kill to protect the people of this circus. I mean that literally. And some advice if you'll take it?"

"What's that, detective?"

"Close the show early. Pack up and move on."

"Why do you say that?"

"Just a hunch. Did you ever see those monster movies with the frightened townsfolk with pitchforks and torches?"

"Yeah."

"You don't want that."

The next day, Syn told Lieutenant Fuller about what he had left out of his official report.

"Are you sure about this, about that, that thing?"

Syn nodded to his lieutenant. "That thing is a dwayyo and his name is Taoke. And even if the wounds and mutilations matched up, I checked the circus's itinerary. The Stone Brothers Circus was nowhere near Harbor City when the first two women were killed."

"I sense a but, Scarecrow."

"Taoke didn't come here alone. He got lost along the way, but it looks like he brought his whole family with him."

"Jesus H. How many?"

"I don't know that. I don't know where they are. And I do know I'm not going to go looking for them. Anything else, Jack?"

Fuller shook his head. "No, that's it. Guess we should keep this between the two of us for now." Syn nodded and got up to leave. As he did, Fuller said. "A mermaid in seashell bra. I'd would have liked to see that."

Syn took Pacifica's cards out of his jacket pocket and flipped them on to Fuller's desk. "Here. Something else I left out of the report."

Chastel's Journal

The newspapers carried the story about the dead clown and dead knife thrower at the circus. Maybe the circus is a place I should hunt. They would cover up what I did.

Chapter Ten

It was near midnight, and it was time for Roy Conner to hunt. He needed cash, he needed thrills, he needed to maybe see some blood, and, if it was a dame and she was pretty enough, he had other needs as well. He knew where to look, knew the places where dark alleys ran off brightly lit streets. Wait for someone to walk by alone, jump out, hold his blade to their throat, and drag them into the shadows. Later he'd walk out alone with whatever they had, whether they wanted to give it up or not.

Laverne Dixon was just getting off work. She worked the busy shift at Elmo's Diner down by the pier — four to midnight. It was always crowded at Elmo's then, but big crowds meant big tips, and Elmo was a nice guy, only making her kick over twenty cents of every dollar. The busser and the cook each got ten cents as well. But with what was left, and the little Elmo paid her, she made enough for a gal to get by. It was a good job, but she wished she didn't have to walk the seven blocks home. The buses stopped coming down to the docks around eleven and yeah, she could call a cab, but what they charged, plus tip, meant that she'd be working an hour for nothing. One cabbie she knew, a guy named Sean, offered an "arrangement," no fares in exchange for once a week in the back seat.

"That way we both get free rides," Sean told her.

Laverne told Sean no, that if she ever got that desperate, she'd go on the stroll and make real money.

"Call me if you do," he said. "I'll be a regular."

Laverne thought of him now and then. He was nice looking and if he hadn't said what he did she might have said yes to a date and, who knows, he might have gotten what he wanted for free.

But Laverne wasn't thinking of Sean that night. All she thought about was how her feet hurt from being on them all day, and how nice it would be to soak them, and how she wished her radio wasn't broken, and how that last guy only left a dime tip on a five-dollar meal, the cheap bastard. The next time he gets the spits. She wasn't thinking about the dark alley she walked by every night on her way home from work. She stopped thinking about that months ago.

Roy found his spot; one he had not used for a while. It wasn't good to go back to a spot too many times. People start avoiding it. The cops start watching. This spot was an alley off Broadway. It led back to another alley that opened out on a small, dark street that was usually quiet at night.

Laverne walked on, counting her steps, counting the blocks. She came to Roy's alley and was halfway across when she was grabbed, pulled far back into the darkness, and thrown face first against a wall. She started to scream but felt the point of a knife against her back and decided not to. A hand roughly felt her ass through her waitress uniform clothes. She heard a whispered "Nice," followed by "Let's walk, bitch."

Roy led the woman through the first alley and into the second. *Here's a good place*, he thought. He'd use her, cut her deep so she'd always remember him, then take her purse and leave. Laverne knew enough not to scream. Instead, she prayed that help would come, prayed that she survived the night.

Again, Laverne was thrown against the wall. A rough hand went up her dress, pulled at her panties.

Then came the growl. The man screamed and Laverne felt him leave her. She turned and saw something… dark.

Roy was pulled from the woman. Sharp claws cut him from behind. He screamed once, lashed out, then screamed again as the knife-edged gauntlets cut into him again and again. As he lay bleeding out in the alley not yet dead, he felt more than saw the Beast kneel, bend over him, and pull apart his wounds. He then felt something and his last thoughts before he died were, *Are those teeth?*

Laverne should have been more scared than she had ever been in her life but instead she was relieved and just a little bit glad that her attacker was getting his.

The Beast did not seem to notice her. It allowed her to watch what it did. When, by the dim alley light, Laverne saw it bend over and rip her attacker apart, she knew she should run. But, entranced, she did not. It bent and seemed to… feed. That's when she turned to run. At her movement, the Beast looked up. Laverne ran back toward the street where she was grabbed. She almost made it.

Chastel's Journal

I learned last night that the thrill of killing a man is no better or worse than killing a woman. And there is no difference in taste between them. Like the last times, I brought some back. Eating there and again when I returned made the dreams and the waking pleasure so much better. I saved some, which I will consume tonight. Then, when it is gone… I will hunt again.

Cooked or raw? I wonder which is better.

Chapter Eleven

The call came in about eight the next morning. A resident of the small, usually quiet street was using the alley to get to the main street to catch the 22 bus to the factory where he worked. His eyes focused ahead, Curtis Reyes walked by the body of Roy Conner without seeing it. The glint of the sun on Laverne Dixon's fallen purse caught his eye. Curtis looked down, saw her body, threw up close to it then ran to find a cop. He did not get to work that day, but his foreman understood. This was Harbor City, and these things happen.

By nine, both alleys were roped off. Beat cops stood watch to keep the public away and the press from lifting the rope and sneaking in for an exclusive look. The ropes didn't stop curious cops from playing looky-loo and by the time Adam Lynch and Jane Higgins arrived any traces of shoeprints had been well trampled.

Surprisingly, Laverne's purse remained untouched. It lay where it had fallen, undisturbed by either Reyes's vomit or venal cops hoping to grab what money it held on the grounds that the victim wouldn't need it anymore. From the bodies, they knew the killer was the Beast and that the case was a red ball. And every cop knew you didn't mess with a red ball.

By unspoken agreement, Higgins first went to look over Laverne's body while Lynch went to Conner's. Higgins knew that the eyes of most of the patrol cops were on her. Not because she was a raving beauty but because she was a woman. They were waiting to see how she'd react to the bloody, savaged corpse. Would she turn pale, look away, throw up? Higgins could hear them thinking, making mental bets that, yeah, she probably would. Yes, the sight of death, this kind of death, was disturbing but Higgins had seen it before and would see it again and the only truly disturbing thing about it was that it never really disturbed her.

Give them a show, she told herself. Looking for a dry spot on the alley floor, she knelt by the corpse and took a long look at what the beast had done to the beauty. She memorized the cuts, the slash marks, and inside the body, noting what was there and what wasn't so she'd have a visual reference when she read Dr. Cruz's report. She longed for the day when crime scenes would be photographed in color, knowing that was probably years if not decades away.

Higgins stood, stepped back from the body, then visually searched the surrounding area. Blood stains splattered on the wall didn't tell her anything she didn't already know, that the woman had been killed where she was found. Taking cotton gloves from her coat pocket she carefully picked up the purse.

The purse was made of black cloth. No prints there. The clasp was shiny metal. Maybe prints on it. She held it up to the light and moved it around but didn't see any visible ones. *Let the lab guys handle it,* she thought deciding not to look inside. *Whoever she is, she can go without a name for a few hours more.*

She was done. She looked down the alley, saw Lynch walking toward her. His eyes trailed the ground, looking for possible evidence. She walked his way. They passed each other without a word, just nodding. They'd compare notes and share observations later. She, too, kept her eyes on the ground, as much to avoid stepping in any blood as to look for evidence.

It was the same thing with the male victim. Cuts and slashes, a blood-stained wall, some organs missing from the body, male cops waiting for her to fail and prove their prejudices. Instead of a purse, a knife lay near the body. A proper-sized one too, and not a switchblade like the punks carried. Maybe prints, probably the victim's. Maybe blood, hopefully from the Beast. Not that the lab could do anything with blood other to say "No, it's not that guy" or "Maybe it's this guy."

This victim had a name, Roy Conner. Higgins knew him, had met him her first week on the beat. He had been the one chosen to test her, to challenge her, to send her back to writing parking tickets. When he put his hands on her she kneed him in the balls then broke his nose with her stick. No one on the streets bothered her after that.

It was Lynch's case, so he was the one to tell the crime lab what evidence to collect (not that they needed telling) and to give the okay for the ME people to tag and bag the bodies. After the scene was clear, they stopped at a greasy spoon and talked evidence and dead bodies over burgers, fries, and coffee.

Back in the Homicide Office, Lynch and Higgins wrote their report, her narrating, him typing — she was faster and more accurate but there was no way she was going to be seen as anyone's secretary. Once it was turned in, Fuller reviewed it then called the squad together for a briefing which was attended not only by the incoming shift but by Fuller's boss George Robeson, Captain of Detectives.

"Male victim is Roy Conner," Lynch said, "a low-life mugger and robber I think some of you have heard of."

"I know Jane has," Ritchie called out. There was general laughter. The story of the first week of the first female beat cop had been told and retold.

"The female victim is Laverne Dixon," Lynch continued. "She had a pay envelope from Elmo's Diner in her purse so I guess Higgins will be taking me out to dinner tonight." More laughter and even more when Higgins said,

"You're taking me. I sprang for lunch."

Lynch went on. "These two looked the same as the first three, only worse. In addition to there being two of them, what was done to the bodies seemed worse, like they were... well, I'll let the ME decide what was done. Dr. Cruz will have her report tomorrow morning, and the lab will have their photos and the results of what they got off the purse. That's it for now except we'll need someone from the evening tour to coordinate the patrol canvas."

Up until now, Syn had been leaning against the far wall, listening. There was something about what Lynch said, how he said it, that made Syn say, "I'll do it." As he said it, he realized that he needed to get out, needed to look at the alleys at night, to get a feel for the hunting ground while it was somewhat fresh. Maybe it was from meeting that dway at the circus.

Syn wondered where the Stone Brothers Circus was. He made a mental note to find out and make sure that Taoke remained with his new pack.

"Good idea," Fuller said. "Keep it all on one squad. Report tomorrow morning."

As the briefing broke up Higgins said. "You might as well eat dinner with us, Syn. After all, Lynch is buying. We'll fill you in and you can tell us all about that mermaid you met at the circus."

"Laverne Dixon was well-liked at Elmo's Diner," Lynch reported at the morning briefing. "Never any problems with the staff or customers. She left at her usual time. No one followed her."

"No one *saw* anyone follow her," Higgins quietly corrected.

Lynch shot her a look. He did not like being corrected and even less in front of a roomful of detectives.

"Yes, well, Scarecrow, what do you have?" Fuller quickly asked before Lynch did. Lynch had a way of taking over a meeting as if he was the one in charge.

From his usual spot leaning against the far wall, Syn said, "Nothing from the canvas, but this is Harbor City. Unless she's on the stroll or acting crazy, no one takes notice." He paused, then, "I walked the scene."

"At night?" Detective Chris Lee asked loudly. "What if the Beast had shown up?"

"Too bad for the Beast then," Higgins said. Some people laughed. Some just nodded. Others looked at Syn, then Lynch, then back to Syn and wondered if the right man was running the investigation.

From his spot in the back, Syn saw this. *Word about me must be getting around*, he thought. "The killer hasn't struck twice in the same place."

"Yet," Higgins reminded him.

Syn nodded at her caution and went on. "It's a perfect hunting ground. Dark alleys and side streets, one path leading into another. A stranger could get lost. Almost like the woods outside the city."

"Where the wild things are."

Used to be, Syn thought, *and maybe they still are*. He'd been putting it off, but maybe it was time to revisit the mountain.

There was a knock, then the door to the meeting room opened. A uniformed policewoman came in and handed Lt. Fuller a folder. On her way out she looked at Higgins in admiration and a little envy.

Fuller read the report. "Dismissed," he said, then added, "Higgins, Syn, Lynch—my office."

The lieutenant sat behind his desk, his three detectives in front of it. "This is Cruz's report. She came in early this morning to finish it. You can read it for yourselves, but the gist is that they were cut deep and bled out. The doc matched the marks made on the bones to those she found on Rose Donavan. They're identical. So yeah, these two were killed by the Beast. And there's something new. This time it looks like the killer took a few bites from each victim and, here I'll quote, 'Given evidence of port-mortem feeding, it is possible that organ removal in these and previous cases was for the purpose of later consumption.'

"Cruz goes on the write that 'the severity of the wounds indicate that the killer is likely bestial in nature. It is tall, bipedal, and extremely powerful. A predatory beast currently unrecognized by science cannot be ruled out.'"

Fuller let it all sink in. Then addressed Syn, "Any of this sound familiar, Scarecrow?"

Syn stood, stretched his long frame, and sat back down. "It does bring back memories." Memories of that terrible time during prohibition when the dwayyo, urged on by a blood-thirsty young man, attacked the Holden roadhouse and killed and devoured most of the people inside. Memories of a battle on a mountaintop, protecting snallygaster chicks from a dwayyo attack. Just him and a shotgun. Had there been one more…

"You okay, Scarecrow?"

"Like I said, Lieutenant, memories."

"What the hell are you talking about?" Lynch loudly demanded to know. Higgins thought she knew. She'd heard stories about the tall, slender man sitting beside her. *Guess they were true*, she thought.

"Well?" Fuller asked.

"Cruz must have gotten a look at Taoke at the circus, probably recognized him for what he is. Maybe that's where she got the idea. But it wasn't him, it's not him. Couldn't be him. The Stone Brothers were nowhere near here when the first attack occurred and have been set up on the Timonium Fairgrounds near Baltimore for the past few days. And yes, I verified it. I had a buddy with the Baltimore County PD check. The Big Bad Wolf never left his pack."

Lynch was quiet but by no means calm. "Circus, Big Bad Wolf," he said, then worked it out. "You mean that… thing in the freak show was really a goddam monster?"

"Tell 'em, Syn."

At Fuller's order he did. When he was done Higgins and Lynch just sat in their seats aghast. "It's possible that some of the pack survived the storm. If so, they've established a den in Corbet Woods. But whoever or whatever the killer is, it's likely not the dwayyo. They hunt in packs and devour their prey where it falls. If it were the dway, the streets of Harbor City would be covered in blood and mostly eaten bodies."

"But," Lynch went on. "Aren't these... monsters dangerous? Shouldn't they be hunted down and destroyed?"

"Yes, they're dangerous," Syn agreed. "But no more than bears, wolves, or other predators if you invade their territory. As for hunting them, anyone who tries to take them on their own ground will have as much luck as the French are having in Indochina with the Viet Minh. Let's concentrate on the killer. Higgins, you said there was a knife found. Any blood on it?"

Fuller answered. "Cruz tested it. Her result was inconclusive."

"Meaning it wasn't human." To Syn, it appeared as if Lynch was ready to marry the idea of a non-human killer.

"Lynch," snapped Fuller. "Remember you're a detective. Inconclusive means no conclusions. Now here's how we'll play it. You and Higgins will work the case following usual procedures. Syn, you cover the monster angle. I'm sure you have... contacts. We go at this hard until there's a break. And not a word of this conversation leaves this room. Understood?" The three detectives nodded. "Okay then. Go solve some crime."

Chastel's Journal

Raw is better.

Chapter Twelve

Despite Fuller's best attempts, the autopsy reports on Roy Conner and Laverne Dixon were leaked to the press. There was no chance they wouldn't be. More people than just Dr. Cruz and the four detectives knew about it and a story about a monster was too good not to share. It grew in the telling until there were monsters stalking the streets of Harbor City hunting for victims to satisfy their desire for human flesh and blood. Or so it was reported on the radio news and in the Harbor City newspapers. Artists' renditions, one more lurid than the next, were included in the morning and evening tabloids.

Once the news broke, Mayor William Gibson called the police commissioner, who called Chief of Police Stockbridge, who called Captain of Detectives Robeson, who called Fuller. The topic of these conversations was basically, "Something needs to be done." What this something was and how it was to be done was never mentioned.

There was talk — by members of the city council, by radio commentators, and by self-appointed public guardians, as well as editorials in the papers — of calling in the State Police to patrol the streets, and of forming a militia to hunt and eliminate these creatures, even though no one knew for sure what these creatures looked like or where they could be found.

Well, some people knew. Theodore Syn knew, Detectives Lynch and Higgins knew, and Lt. Fuller knew. Presumably, Dr. Dela Cruz had strong suspicions based on her glimpse of the "Big Bad Wolf."

"It won't take long before someone remembers the old legends and stories," Fuller said to Syn over beers in 10-44, a cop bar not far from police headquarters, "especially the one about the massacre at the Holden House during the Roadhouse Wars." Fuller drained his beer, called for another, then looked at Syn, hope in his eyes. "Please tell me that's all that is, a story."

Syn dashed Fuller's hope by saying, "Yeah, a true story. One of the gang bosses somehow got the dway riled up and put them on the hunt. People died and were eaten, and it would have been worse if the Snallygasters had not intervened."

"Snallygasters?" Fuller asked. Syn nodded. "Do I want to know?" Syn shook his head. "Dammit. Scarecrow, Lynch and Higgins are good detectives, two of the best, for all that Higgins is a woman. Hell, maybe because she's a woman and maybe we should get more dicks without dicks on the force. If the killer's human they'll find him, or them. But..."

"What do you need me to do, Jack?"

"If there's something out there, find it and find out if what Dela Cruz and the papers are saying could be true."

"And if it is?"

"Then lead the hunt yourself. You're the only one who can..."

"I'll look into it. I'll need some time." Fuller nodded. "As for the hunt..." Syn left the subject open.

That night after he and Cara were in bed, he asked his wife, "Feel like taking a trip? Jericho is old enough to take care of himself."

"Where to?"

"Up to Sandy Point, maybe across the bay."

"You're going to see Chessie. It's about the killings, isn't it." Syn said that it was. Cara thought for a moment. "Why not? What with Jericho in the house we need some time alone, and I like Chessie. For all her size she's a gentile creature. Not like the other ones. I know, they're sort of your cousins. You're not going to see them, are you?" There was concern in her voice. Her husband's cousins, the Snallygasters, scared her. She had met them once and vowed never again.

"I might." Which was Syn's way of saying he probably would.

"If you do, don't you dare take Jericho. Let the stories you've told him stay just stories. What else?"

"We'll have to go to Crisfield. There have been some reports of strange deaths and killings coming from there."

"When are we leaving?"

"Tomorrow morning."

"Then we'll both need our sleep tonight. There'll be time for anything else during the trip."

Probably one of my last ferry rides, Syn thought as he and Cara crossed the Chesapeake Bay. There was serious talk about building a bridge to connect Maryland's Eastern Shore with the greater part of the state. During the crossing, both he and Cara sensed Chessie's presence, although they did not speak until the first night Syn and Cara were on the other side.

Chessie told Syn about the dway's swim across the bay, about the storm, and how she rescued the one called Taoke. *Some I could not save,* she told Syn. *More made it safely to shore.*

When Syn asked, *Where?* Chessie showed him. He then asked, *Was there any trouble on this side before the crossing?*

Men attacked them. They fought back. There was death on both sides.

Syn and Cara took a room in a bayside hotel near the water. He left her there to enjoy local shopping and talks with Chessie and checked in with the Crisfield Police. There he got the human side of the story, of how monsters had attacked and eaten a man named Trace Norton and his horse Barney and how those who tracked the monsters were set upon and mostly killed.

"I hear you folk in Harbor City are having monster problems of your own," Sheriff Dudley Austin said. "Guess that's why you're here."

Syn nodded, thinking, *News travels fast,* and knew that it would not be long before the story of the Crisfield Massacre, as it was locally known, traveled to Harbor City.

The crossing west on the ferry *Dani* was at night. There were stars and a full moon. The ferry was not that crowded. When Syn suggested to Cara that they find some shadows she said, "Not that I wouldn't like to, but let's wait. I'm sure there'll be a nice hotel once we get off."

The day Syn got back to work he reported what he had learned to Lt. Fuller. "Cara and I got off the ferry near where Chessie said the dwayyo probably ended up. I worked my way up from there, talking to cops and locals. There were no reports of strange beasts killing and eating people but there were sightings of 'wolf-like' creatures, 'like out of that Lon Chaney movie' one person said. There were also attacks on pigs, cows, and horses and some pets went missing."

"And did you check out Corbet Woods to see if these dwayyo have returned to their old hunting grounds?" Syn shook his head. "Why not?"

"Do you see 'stupid' written on my forehead? Anyway, there's no need. There's game in those woods. Has been for years. If Chessie's right about the pack size, there's plenty to keep them going."

"Doesn't matter. Thanks to the press and the politicians looking to score votes for the next election, the damage is done. People think there are monsters so there are monsters. Next killing, there'll be another public outcry that 'something should be done.' And that 'something' will be a monster hunt."

Chapter Thirteen

It was not yet time. The dreams were still sharp and the morning pleasure so good I sometimes cried out. Still, I had to venture forth. One or two more deaths will panic the city and set them on a false trial. Old tales of Gevaudan tell of how family crimes were blamed on our brothers the beasts and so never punished by man. It is time that, like before, the pack suffers for the sins which give so much pleasure.

One more sleep, one more awakening, then when the night fell, I went out to do what I had to.

I found my prey on a dark street. We were alone. Like the second woman, he was about to go into his house. With my hands in my deep pockets, I slid them into my claws and waited for the door to open. I rushed forward, pushed him inside. He screamed and we fell, me on top. I growled and started slashing, all the time listening for other sounds, other people in the house. I heard nothing. He quickly fell silent and stopped struggling. He was not yet dead when I opened him and began to feed. Alone, I took my time.

When daylight came, I was home, having carried away the choicest meats. I slept deep, dreaming of my kill, dreaming that it was a family. When I woke up the pleasure came fast and hard.

**THE BEAST STRIKES AGAIN
DEATH STALKS HARBOR CITY
YOU'RE NOT EVEN SAFE IN YOUR HOMES
SLAUGHTER ON POTEE STREET**

After a neighbor found Martin Buckner's body in his home, these headlines and more stoked the fear and panic. Lillie Woods was walking by Martin's house when she noticed his door stood open. No one in Harbor City did that and worried that her neighbor was sick she went inside. As she walked across the living room to turn on a light, she stepped in something wet. When the light came on, she saw that the something wet was Martin. Her screams alerted more neighbors, one of whom called the police.

Detectives Lynch and Higgins did not need the ME to tell them that Martin Buckner had suffered the same fate as the other victims of the Beast. Only more so. After all, the Beast had had time.

"So, what do you think, Lynch?" Higgins asked her partner. "Did he scoop and eat or did he kneel and chow down?"

Adam Lynch had always thought he was tough, that he had seen the worst one human being could do to another, that he could handle anything.

That day proved him wrong. Looking down at Martin Buckner's savaged remains in the harsh light of a 100-watt incandescent bulb, Lynch felt his breakfast begin a return trip. *No*, he told himself, struggling not to vomit, *not here. Not in front of... a woman.* Blowing his guts in front of male officers would be embarrassing enough but in front of Higgins would be worse, especially since she did not seem to be at all affected by the sight.

"Do not throw up," Higgins ordered. "If you do, then so will I. We'll both contaminate the body and Dr. Cruz will put us on the table next to this one."

The hardest thing Adam Lynch may have ever done was to steel himself and swallow his breakfast for the second time that day.

"Shall we leave Mr. Buckner for the Crime Lab and the ME's people?" Higgins asked. Lynch could only nod his agreement.

Once outside, the detective saw the mass of people, particularly newspaper reporters and photographers, crowding the police line established on either end of Potee St. Looking up, Higgins saw a few photographers taking pictures from the opposite side roof.

"This is bad," Lynch said once he could speak again. He needed a drink, a strong one, either something distilled or last night's station house coffee, to get the taste of once-eaten, twice-swallowed sausage and eggs out of his mouth.

"And you know something, Lynch?"

"What, Higgins?"

"It's only going to get worse. But there's one good thing."

"What's that?"

"It's an inside scene. Prints, trace evidence, all that Sherlock Holmes stuff the crime unit does that makes us look good."

"Yeah," he said, not believing her for a minute. Which was okay because she didn't believe it either.

Mayor Gibson waited until Dr. Cruz had finished Martin's autopsy and confirmed that not only did his death match those of the other five victims but that parts of his body had been consumed prior to the killer leaving the scene. In addition, other parts had been removed, "torn from the body" were her exact words, for possible consumption later. With this information at hand, the mayor declared a state of emergency and imposed an eleven P.M. curfew. Then he asked the governor to send in the state police to help the HCPD enforce the curfew. He also put out a call for "experienced fighters" to volunteer for a militia to "hunt down the monster responsible for these brutal attacks."

"Doesn't look good, Scarecrow," Jack Fuller said over beers in the 10-44.

"I don't know, Jack. No criminals or working girls roaming the streets. Bars, nightclubs, blind pigs, gambling dens, the houses—all shut down. Harbor City might just become respectable."

"That will be the day. I've already heard that the houses on Convent Way are offering 'sleepover specials' at no more than triple the usual price."

Syn *humphed*. "At that rate, men might decide to stay home with their wives. Could be a good thing."

There was a pause. Both men refilled their mostly empty mugs.

"How soon do you think before the hunt starts?" Syn asked.

"Maybe a week. The governor has to review the mayor's request and decide if committing the State Police is in his best interest. In the end, I think he'll approve the request. Then this militia will have to be mustered and a plan of attack drawn up."

"I already know the plan. The militia will be given the order to go into Corbet Woods south of the city and kill everything that moves except each other. They'll patrol a section of woods from the access road to the mountain then back again and start over with another section until they've covered all of it."

"What do you think will happen?"

"Armed men—hunters and veterans trained in various kinds of warfare—against top-level predators on their home ground who think of humans as part of their food chain? Nothing good. Meanwhile, the Beast will still be among us. He'll strike sometime after the sun goes down and be in bed by eleven, probably with a juicy, meaty bedtime snack. And when he kills again, and again, and again, the mayor, the governor, and everyone else will say 'At least we tried' then blame the cops for not stopping him."

"And what will you be doing?"

"Unless you need me, Jack, I might take some time to go camping. Clear my head and try to figure this whole thing out."

Chapter Fourteen

Theodore Syn had not been to the hills of Corbet County since just before the war started. He went to say farewell to his "cousins" Kona and Forra before the two great snallygasters settled into what might be a decades-long sleep. They had raised several broods, some of which contained part of Syn's essence. He thought of this as he made camp on the mountaintop and wondered just where Kona and Forra were hidden. He thought of his nieces and nephews, the closest of which was in Frederick County and the rest scattered throughout the high places along the east coast. How many times, he wondered, was a snallygaster in flight mistaken for a hawk, eagle, or owl?

Syn had come up the back roads well away from the dwayyo hunting grounds. They might still sense him but probably not bother to seek him out. This mountain was taboo, the place of the flying ones. Syn remembered that night:

The dwayyo attacking the roadhouse. Kona and Forra flying off at his request to stop further killing and leaving him to protect their chicks. The dwayyo attacking. There were three, no, two of them after the chicks. Somehow, he had beaten them but it was a close thing.

Syn looked out from the mountain. Harbor City sprawled in the distance, blazing bright. The mayor had ordered every light in the city turned on to lessen the shadows where the Beast could hide. *Damned fool, doesn't he know that it's the light that causes the shadow.*

Syn next looked down into the moonlit woods. *Soon,* he thought, *the eternal struggle of man versus beast will resume again.*

"Poor bastards," he said aloud, not sure if he was talking about the militia or the dwayyo.

Then he looked within himself, quieting his mind of all thoughts except the problem. Was the killer human or beast? He realized that they had only Dela Cruz's word for the latter. *Her professional opinion*, he corrected himself. But still, it should be tested, confirmed by another doctor, maybe one more experienced. His mind strayed, thinking less of Cruz the doctor and Dela the woman. She was beautiful, and alluring, and distracting. Distracting enough that he had not thought of asking for a second opinion until just then.

How could they test her conclusion? No, that was the wrong question. How would *he* test it if had he the skills? After a time, he thought of a way, a terrible way that very much depended on the coming conflict. *Needs must*, he thought, very much aware that not only was the devil behind the wheel but he drove much too fast.

Syn thought of the crime scenes, what had and had not been there. He had walked the alley and been to the house. Nothing left on either scene but the lingering scent of death. Normally he'd review the findings but there was damn little real evidence. Just a knife with the killer's blood, only the results of the blood tests came back inconclusive. *According to Dr. Cruz's tests.*

A yet-unformed idea teased his mind. To let it come he thought of other things. Cara and their life and love together. His nephew Jericho, who wanted to be a cop like his uncle and who had unfortunately inherited his uncle's looks. The first time he saw Chessie and the majesty of that great and gentle (to him at least) serpent. He thought of Kona's embrace and of what he had given the snallygaster and how she had left her mark on him.

Syn's thoughts drifted until there were no thoughts, just peace — the peace of the mountain, the peace of the night, the peace of his mind.

The idea came and it was a good one, crazy and dangerous but good. Syn just didn't know how he was going to get Jack Fuller to agree to it.

Maybe, Syn thought, *I won't tell him.*

Chapter Fifteen

The Militia had its orders. Three squads of twenty, each to search a section of the woods. The rules of engagement were simple. If it's not human and not normal kill it. The commander of the Militia left it to its members to determine the meaning of "not normal."

They went in at dawn, with mist still on the ground and rolling off the mountain.

The pack was about to settle in its den to sleep. Dagr and Inkir taking the first watch when human scent was detected. It was in the air, coming from several directions close to the edge of the woods away from the mountain. Men were coming, many men.

Human packs, Revna decided. *A strong one below us. Weaker packs on either side.* She knew a hunting formation when she sensed one.

As did the other adults and possibly the older youths.

What do they hunt? asked the cub Dag.

Smaller groups of men would sometimes enter the woods in search of smaller game. They were no threat and so came and went unmolested. But three packs of this size? There was only one answer.

Dagr answered Dag. *Us. Revna, we must…*

The pack leader cut off his thoughts. *We must hide. We must scatter, dig down and deep, cover over, stay silent until night. If then the humans have left or are leaving, all will be good.*

And if not, asked the adult Ulfhild.

Then it will be bad for them, for they are creatures of the day, and the night is ours.

To the adults she sent, *We will each take a cub and make sure it does not cry out. If it does, silence it so it will never cry again.*

But… Sindr objected. One of the cubs, Tove, was hers.

The pack comes first, Revna rebuked her. *We can bear more cubs. I will take Tove.*

The pack hid, buried itself, and remained still and hidden even as the men passed close by, unaware of their presence.

The hunters, although the dway would not call them that, spread thinly in a long line, their weapons at the ready. One of them, a young male, came close to where Dagr and the cub Aslog hid. Aslog's excitement was apparent to the older dway as he stirred beneath Dagr.

Easy, he sent to the cub, *stay silent.* Then thought to himself, *How easy it would be to kill this human.* But he did not. Instead, he sent his thoughts into the young man's mind and urged him to move in another direction just before the youth stepped onto the mound that hid the two dway.

They are past, Dagr sent to Revna. *Shall we take them from behind?*

No, the pack leader sent back. *We give them the day and wait for the night.*

After taking a detour into Frederick County, Maryland, Theodore Syn arrived back in Harbor City just as the militia invaded the dwayyo's domain. Without checking in with his lieutenant, he drove straight to the Medical Examiner's Office. Asking for Dr. Lethem, he was directed to the autopsy room where the pathologist was examining the victim of a fatal hit-and-run. On hearing, "Dr. Lethem," he looked up and saw Syn standing at a distance from the examining table.

"I wouldn't have thought the Scarecrow was squeamish."

"I'm not, doctor, I just don't want to contaminate the field."

"There's nothing to contaminate. This man got hit by two tons of Detroit steel," the doctor said. "But thank you for your consideration. How can I help you?"

"It's about Dr. Cruz."

Behind his mask, Lethem gave out a low growl that would have done credit to a dwayyo. "What about her? She's busy briefing Mayor Gibson about her 'monsters'."

"You don't like her very much, do you?"

"There are a lot of people I don't like. Dela Cruz is one of them. I'll leave my reasons to your imagination. Anything I say may be used against me and all that. Now, again, what about her?"

"Have you had occasion to review her autopsies on the Beast's victims?"

"We read each other's reports regularly. It's routine procedure. I found nothing in her reports to cause any concern."

"Have you personally viewed any of the bodies?"

Lethem stopped his examination of the accident victim. He looked over the body, nodded, then quickly but skillfully sewed it up. Stripping off his mask and gown and tossing them into the laundry bin, he asked Syn, "Why?" Then, "No, wait. The so-called Harbor City Militia has marched off to war against Cruz's monsters, assuming they exist. You think they do and are expecting casualties on both sides. And, assuming you are right, this would provide an opportunity to compare known causes of death to Cruz's monster theory. How am I doing, detective?"

Syn smiled. "As you said, anything I say, etc. For now, I'm asking you to cast your professional eye over the latest victim of the Beast, assuming it's still here."

"It is. No next of kin and too torn up for the medical school. It's in storage waiting for enough John and Jane Does to make a trip to Potter's Field worthwhile."

"Well, doctor, since Dr. Cruz is with the mayor..."

"You're right, detective. Let's go check out her work."

The day ended without the militia accomplishing anything beyond frightening the wildlife they expected to be there. It did not find any trace of monsters. As evening fell and before it became too dark to see, the captains of the three squads called a halt and ordered their men to set up camp. In the morning, they would continue the search until they reached the mountain, then shift position and work their way back toward Harbor City.

The men were tired and discouraged. They had been expecting action and adventure, a fight with the crazed beasts terrorizing their city, a confrontation they were sure to win given their superior firepower. Instead, they got a day-long, uneventful hike in the woods with no stories to tell when they returned home.

Three separate fires burned brightly in the woods, marking each camp's position. Around these fires, men talked and bragged. They groused about the mission and what a waste of time it was. Some suggested that instead of going on to the mountain they simply turn around and go home come morning. Inwardly, one of the three captains agreed but instead said, "Enough of that talk. We continue the mission."

Guards were set at each camp, four men patrolling the perimeter, relief every two hours. The rest of the militia settled in or on their sleeping bags. Tired, most quickly fell asleep.

Come the darkness, the dwayyo uncovered. Like the men, the pack divided into three groups, three elders or youths per group with one cub each, plus Tove at her mother's side. The campfires marked their prey's position, but even at a distance the light bothered their eyes and so the dway relied on their senses of hearing and smell to lead them to the men who dared to invade their land.

Revna kept them linked to each other. When they got close enough, when they could smell the odor of the prey, when they could hear the snoring of the sleeping men who thought they were safe and the *trud, trud, trud* of those who patrolled the camp she sent, *Now is the time.*

As one, the pack sent out thoughts of fear and lassitude toward its prey.

Loud growling alerted the guards. However, most had failed to keep their eyes away from the campfire and so had little or no night vision. They did not know that the dway were among them until they felt claws tear into their chests and back and sharp teeth in their necks. The growls and their screaming awoke the other militia members. In their dwayyo-induced panic, some ran while others grabbed their rifles and began firing randomly. These were the ones who lay on top of their sleeping bags. The ones who slept inside got tangled up and before they could free themselves and find their weapons, the dway were among them — tearing, biting, killing.

Yrsa was hit by a bullet. He killed the human closest to him, tearing out his throat and drinking his blood. He then collapsed.

The surviving members of the militia fled in all directions into the darkness. The dway allowed them to go, but for one that Revna caught and held, uninjured, in her sharp-clawed paws.

The woods grew suddenly quiet except for the moans of the human wounded.

Silence them, Revna ordered. Claws slashed and the moaning stopped.

Pack Leader, sent Ulfhild, *come. It is Yrsa.* Revna went to him, dragging with her the helpless human.

Zachary Crane was eighteen. He had enlisted in the Army as soon as he could but had not seen any action. He was not even sent overseas. He was considered a veteran by all but himself and those who had fought and bled. He had joined the Harbor City Militia to make up for what he had missed.

Now he was sorry he did. He had shat and pissed himself. He shook uncontrollably in the grip of a creature he was sure would haunt his nightmares for the rest of his days.

Suddenly in his mind he heard, *Calm.* To his surprise he did. Then, *You are safe. You will not be harmed.*

Revna needed this human, needed him to deliver a message. That is why she calmed his thoughts. Looking deeper into his mind, she found that he had been one of the few who had fought back.

You were brave, you fought the pack, she sent as she marched him over to where Yrsa lay.

It was clear to all, even to Crane, that Yrsa was about to leave the pack. *Witness what you have done*, Revna sent to Crane. She meant what he and his pack of humans had done. If he wished to claim the kill that was his affair.

Yrsa lasted until it was almost morning, facing his painful death without a whimper. Finally, he breathed his last

Only once Yrsa had left the pack did Revna turn toward the human.

Why? she sent. From his mind she pulled the answer, what he knew about the Beast of Harbor City.

Revna opened her mouth. "Huh, huh, huh," she laughed at the story.

We will let you go. When you return, tell your pack leaders that it is not the dwayyo who are doing this. If it were, we would be feeding every night, not like this Beast. Tell them not to send any more hunters, unless they wish them to die as well. Then Revna thought. She thought of the viciousness of men, how they destroy that which they fear. She pictured the woods on fire, fires set by men so as to destroy the pack. Again, they would have to move, unless …

And tell them to send me the Scarecrow.

Chapter Sixteen

The surviving members of the Harbor City Militia emerged from the woods one by one. As they reported to the Command Center, they told of being ambushed in the night by growling, unseen beasts who walked on two legs. Only a few of the survivors were wounded—some with broken limbs from falls incurred during their panicky, nighttime flight. Two had bullet wounds from friendly fire. Except for one man, none gave any coherent descriptions of their attackers, only "monsters in the dark."

Zachary Crane was one of the last to arrive. The dwayyo had given him time to wash himself and clean his shame from his clothing. They gave him time to eat and rest. When he was ready, two youths escorted him to the edge of the woods. Remaining out of sight, they watched until his fellow men greeted him. When they questioned him, he talked of werewolves that spoke to him with their minds, who denied attacking people in the city, who warned against further invasion, and who asked for someone or something called "Scarecrow."

Theodore Syn watched from his desk in the far corner of the Homicide Office as Captain Robeson and Chief Stockbridge passed by on their way to Jack Fuller's office. Next came the Police Commissioner and Mayor Gibson. He had heard about the disastrous raid into the woods. It had gone exactly the way he had feared. He had not heard about Zachary Crane and the message he had carried. Still, he was not surprised when he was called into his lieutenant's office.

It was crowded inside. The mayor had commandeered the lieutenant's chair. The commissioner and chief sat on either side of him. With no remaining chairs, Fuller and his captain were forced to stand.

Syn did likewise, as usual leaning against the wall on the latchside of the office door.

"I take it you're Detective Syn, also known as the Scarecrow?" Gibson asked almost as soon as Syn entered the room.

"Yes, sir, I am," Syn said, not bothering to straighten as he answered.

"You will address the mayor as 'Your Honor,' bellowed Chief Robeson, "and stand up straight when speaking to him, detective."

Syn's only reply to the chief was to raise his eyebrows. Turning toward the mayor, he asked, "What do you want to know—your honor?" Syn's somewhat delayed "your honor" was more mocking than respectful. The mayor ignored him.

"What do you know about these, these dwayyo?"

Syn could have spent most of the day and into the night telling the assembled officials all that he knew. Instead, he simply said, "They are bipedal, wolf-like predators. They travel in packs, are intelligent and self-aware, and communicate mostly by thought."

"Tell me, Detective Syn, have you any idea why these so-called intelligent, self-aware creatures would be asking for you?"

Syn looked at Fuller who nodded. He looked at the others in the room all of whom looked back, their faces full of doubt and suspicion as if he were the dway's pack leader or even the Beast himself. He had an idea why the dway's leader would want to meet with him, but it was not one he wished to share. He also had his own suspicions, that, except for Jack Fuller, the men in Fuller's office were planning to use him as a judas goat.

"I have no id…" Syn's eyes suddenly opened in apparent surprise and looked toward a far corner of the room. Except for Fuller's all other eyes followed his stare. So it was that only Jack Fuller saw him quickly open the office door and slip out.

Syn was halfway down the stairs before anyone in Fuller's office could react. He made it to the motor pool and commandeered a large, unmarked car before word went out to find and detain Detective Theodore Syn, aka the Scarecrow. This word was also radioed to the militia command post that was still receiving the stragglers who had gotten lost in the woods.

Syn expected this is what they would do. He drove west out of the city, then traveled the back roads until he came to the same route he had taken before. Driving the car as far as it could go, he again ascended the mountain. There he sat, opened his mind, and sent his thoughts out toward the dwayyo.

It was shortly after sunset when Theodore Syn heard the dwayyo coming. He suspected that they allowed him to hear them so he would be aware of their approach. *I hope that means they're not going to kill me,* he thought. He then thought of his shotgun, hidden out of sight but within easy reach. *Not that it will do me any good if there's more than one of them.*

There were three of them, a female and two males. The female stood in the center and slightly forward. The pack leader.

Greetings, he thought toward them. *I am the Scarecrow.*

I am Revna, the pack leader sent. *With me are Inkir and Ulfhild.*

Why did you ask for me?

You humans came into our hunting ground. We killed many and the rest fled. Revna waited for Syn to reply. When he did not... *They will come again, won't they?*

Yes, Syn said. *We destroy what we fear.* He sent all three images of war—wholesale death, killing machines, aerial bombardment. *If we do this to our own kind, we will not hesitate to do the same to you.*

Syn had anticipated something like this and so had come prepared. *You must leave these woods.*

We must leave, Revna agreed. *But where can we go?*

Syn realized that that was why they were meeting with him. He knew from Taoke that they had heard of him and hoped he would have an answer. He had anticipated this and had made preparations.

Go north, go tonight. He sent her the location. *I am of the Flying Ones. A member of my flock will grant you space but only if you vow peace between your pack and her flock.* When Revna hesitated, he sent, *Have you any other choice?*

She did not. *Very well.*

There is one thing. The humans you killed, where are their bodies? Revna sent this to him. *And did any of the dway leave your pack?* Revna told him of Yrsa.

Leave him in this place. He sent her the location of his car. Again, Revna hesitated. *His body will be respected. I swear this by my flock.*

It will be done, Revna sent. *What honor there is in humans is in you, Scarecrow.*

Thank you. There is one other thing. Syn wondered if he should tell them but decided they had a right to know. *Taoke survived the storm. He has found a new pack. He is content.*

Revna nodded thanks. *Tell him if he ever wishes to return, he is welcome.*

I shall. Now go, Revna, take your pack and lead them to their new home. Go now, travel fast. Travel far before daylight comes.

Syn watched as the three dway stepped back and let the shadows swallow them.

Syn waited in his car when suddenly it rocked as something heavy was placed in its trunk. He got out and checked the contents. He covered the body of the dwayyo, closed the trunk, and drove back toward Harbor City.

Chapter Seventeen

They were waiting for Syn when he arrived at the militia command post. He had radioed them he was coming. He was met by Jack Fuller, Mayor Gibson, and Chief Stockbridge. None were happy with him.

"Syn, what the hell were you doing? Conspiring with your monster friends?" Stockbridge all but shouted at him. "I should have you…"

Syn forestalled whatever the chief was going to do to him and addressed Mayor Gibson. "The dwayyo are gone. They want no war with us, so they've left Corbet Woods."

Gibson looked surprised. "And how did you manage that, detective?" he asked warily.

Syn said calmly, "I'm the Scarecrow, it's what I do," he replied, adding, "Their pack leader also gave me the location of the bodies of the militia."

The chief would not leave things alone. "That's bullshit, Syn. Why should we believe anything you say? We've sent men to the campsites. They report blood but no bodies. What did your monsters do, eat them whole? When this is all over, I'm bringing you up on charges—going AWOL, acting without proper authority, conspiring with, and aiding and abetting… whatever the hell they are. I'll have your badge and, if I can manage it, see you in jail."

"That's enough, Stockbridge," Mayor Gibson said. "This man put his life on the line for us. He deserves a medal, not charges. Now stand down, in fact, leave the area before I reconsider the need to have both a commissioner and a chief of police." He turned his back on Stockbridge. "My apologies, Detective Syn, or should I call you 'Scarecrow'?"

"Whatever you like, Your Honor. Now if you'll excuse me, I'll let the militia commander know where he can find the bodies of his men."

Syn did so, then made a phone call. "Commander Nebel, I've put in a call to the Medical Examiner's Office. Doctor Lethem will be out to formally take charge of the bodies and tell you where they are to be transported."

"This whole thing was a fubar," Nebel replied, "but at least their families will have the cold comfort of being able to bury their loved ones. Personally, and on their behalf, I thank you for what you did."

Syn acknowledged the thanks, then thought back to the call he had just made.

"Dr. Lethem, Theodore Syn here. In reference to what we talked about earlier, I have some bodies for comparison."

"How many, detective?"

"Too many." He explained the situation to Lethem. When the doctor finished swearing, Syn added, "Plus I have the other specimen. When would you like to see that?"

There was a pause. "Tonight, after I leave the command post. Bring the specimen around to the loading and unloading area."

Later that night, Lethem met Syn on the loading dock. "You were right, detective, while the injuries I observed on those men looked similar to those of the Beast's victims and while I'll need to make a more thorough examination, from what I saw I would have to rule out a... dwayyo did you call them, as the Beast. For one thing, the method of devouring was different. On the Beast's latest victims, it seemed to be selective feeding. What I saw out there..." Lethem paused, "...frankly what I saw out there will haunt my dreams for a long time. Here I had thought I'd seen it all. But what I saw was, the best word for it was indiscriminate and opportunistic. Limbs, organs, necks. It appeared that the dwayyo just selected an area at random and continued eating until it was full. As for the wounds left on the uneaten deceased, I can only suppose they were being saved for later. Now I would like to examine the specimen you brought me."

With Lethem's help, Syn moved the body of the dwayyo from the trunk of Syn's car to an examination gurney, then they wheeled it into the autopsy room. The body of Martin Buckner was waiting on another table for a side-by-side comparison.

"What a magnificent beast," Lethem exclaimed when he saw the dwayyo in full light.

"His name is Yrsa and he's not a beast," Syn quietly corrected. "He may not be human, but he and his kind are sentient beings with customs, traditions, and a sense of honor."

"And a taste for human flesh."

"All flesh, doctor. The dway do not discriminate. Now, what can you tell me?"

"Look at the wounds on Buckner. All nice and even, almost straight lines. Now, look at the claws of the dwayyo. The wounds they would leave would be more splayed out. I observed this on the bodies of the men at the command post. I think the wounds would be the same if left by any non-human predator."

"Your conclusion, doctor?"

"That Martin Buckner and his fellow victims were killed by a human trying to simulate the marks of a beast."

"Can you make that official?"

"Not yet, not without admitting I had access to the body of this magnificent creature. I don't suppose…"

"I gave my word that the body of Yrsa would be honorably disposed of."

"Would fire be honorable? We have a cremation oven for the body parts we remove and are finished with."

Syn nodded and Yrsa's body was given to the flames. As it burned, Lethem surprised Syn by praying, "Oh God, I do not know if the dwayyo Yrsa knew You but You, Who knows when each sparrow falls and the number of hairs on our heads, surely knew him. Please receive him into whatever paradise awaits his kind and grant him and his pack Your peace. Amen."

"Amen," echoed Syn. "Nicely done, doctor."

"Thank you, detective, now help me clean up."

As they two erased all signs of their unauthorized and highly improper night's work, Lethem said, "I'll wait until I have examined more of the fallen militia before issuing my report. You know, detective, I cannot imagine why Dr. Cruz even suspected a non-human creature caused these murders. Maybe she wanted the killer to be a monster."

A sudden thought occurred to Syn. *Or she needed him to be.*

She needed him to be. Now, why would I think that? Syn wondered on his way home. He put the thought aside. He'd go home and get a good night's rest. Tomorrow he'd make his report. Lethem's findings did not mean there wasn't a monster, just that whoever or whatever it was wasn't a dway. That only left the idea that had come to him on the mountain. It was crazy, perhaps the craziest thing ever, and this from a man who had been involved with snallygasters, dwayyo, and sea serpents. But it wasn't something he could, or should, do on his own.

I'll talk it over with Cara tonight, he decided.

Jericho was out. Cara was not in the mood to talk. It was only when they rested that he told her of his idea.

"You're right, it's as crazy as a bagful of squirrels. But what else is new?" she said. "And it's worth a try. Just promise me something, Ted?"

"What, Cara."

"After this, and except for those who are, well, friends and family, no more monsters."

"I'll do my best, dear, I'll do my best."

The next day, after typing up and giving his report to Fuller, Syn took Lynch and Higgins aside and told them his plan.

"That's the craziest, goddam plan I've ever heard," Lynch said.

"But it might work," Higgins replied. "Edmond Locard, Lyon, France, just before the war. Every contact leaves a trace."

"And sometimes that trace is something we can't see, or sense. The only question is how long does that trace linger?" Syn asked. "Lynch, it's your case. It's your call."

Lynch thought a while, then, "What the hell? We don't have anything else to go on. And we can't rely on getting lucky before another body or two drops. Let's try it. If it works, Higgins and I will get the credit. If it doesn't, we can always blame you."

"Great," Syn said. "Now all we need is a patrol wagon."

Higgins spoke up. "Maggie in Motor Pool is a friend. She can get us one."

Syn stuck his head into Fuller's office. The lieutenant was on the phone. "Higgins, Lynch, and I have a lead on the Beast. We may be gone for a while."

The lieutenant paused his conversation. "How long?" Syn answered with a shrug. "Do I want to know why?"

"Not in the least."

"Okay, just be careful, Scarecrow."

Three in the front seat of a patrol wagon was a tight fit. Syn drove to Baltimore where they picked up the York Road. After stopping for lunch, Higgins took the wheel and drove them into Pennsylvania and the York County Fairgrounds. She drove past a banner advertising "The Stone Brothers' Traveling Circus, Carnival, and Natural Odditys Exhibition" and parked in the lot marked "Circus Folk only."

"You want to what?!" Evan Stone's shout almost rattled the walls of his office trailer.

"We want to borrow the Big Bad Wolf. It's in reference to the Beast murders in Harbor City."

Stone looked at the three detectives suspiciously. He had had a lot of dealings with police of all kinds during his many years in the circus. Most of them cost him money in the form of bribes, permits, and trumped-up fines. Few of his experiences had been pleasant ones. He immediately came to the wrong conclusion.

"You're not planning to frame him for the murders, are you? Because if you are..."

"If we were," Higgins interrupted, "he would be dead or locked up by now. No, Detective Syn has cleared the dwayyo of any involvement in the Beast murders. What we need... Taoke, was it... for is as a sort of expert witness. If he can help us, all the right people will be told how helpful the Stone Brothers Circus was in closing the case."

Evan Stone was raised in the circus. He had seen many strange, bizarre, and wondrous things. But he had never met or even seen a female police officer, much less a police detective. Her rarity fascinated him and for this reason he was inclined to believe her.

"Okay, you can talk to him after the last show. If he agrees, he's yours. Just bring him back."

"If he's willing," Syn said, thinking of Taoke's old pack, hopefully now in their new den in Frederick. *When it's all over*, Syn promised himself, *Taoke gets to make his choice.*

They met in the Big Bad Wolf's tent. Lynch and Higgins were, at first, reluctant to approach the dway, especially since the cage door was, at Syn's request, open. Instead, they stayed close to the entrance of the tent.

Even Syn could feel their fear. Taoke put them at ease with calming thoughts.

It is okay, he sent, startling them even more when they "heard" his thoughts, despite Syn having told them to expect it. *You are of the Scarecrow's pack. The Scarecrow is a friend of my pack.* Taoke's thoughts made it clear that his pack was the circus. *Pack leader Stone tells me that you need my help. You are safe. Besides, I have already eaten.*

Taoke followed this with a "Huh, huh, huh."

"Dwayyo humor," Syn explained to his worried comrades. Then to Taoke, *There is a beast hunting in our city. We would like you to help us find it.*

If I can, Scarecrow. How can I help?

If you are willing, we would like you to come with us to Harbor City. We will take you to different hunting grounds to see if there is a scent in common to them that does not belong to the three of us.

Will you return me to my pack?

Yes, if that is what you wish.

Why would I not wish to be with my pack?

Syn did not answer. Instead, he sent, *Let's go then.* To Higgins and Lynch, he said, "It's on. I'll ride in the back with Taoke."

As they were getting into the wagon, Evan Stone came up carrying a cooler packed with ice and raw meat. "It's for Grimm. He's a growing boy and might get hungry."

The ride back to Harbor City was uneventful. Taoke sent to Syn, *It will be good to hunt again*, then went to sleep. Syn tried to sleep, but the dreams of the dwayyo kept entering his thoughts. They were strange and, even though he did not understand them, very disturbing.

They took the last scene first, the house in which Martin Buckner was killed and partially eaten. Thanks to the curfew, Potee St. was dark and empty when the detectives pulled up. Lynch and Higgins got out of the patrol wagon to make sure it stayed that way while Syn broke the police seal and hustled Taoke into the house. Lynch joined him while Higgins kept watch outside.

There is death here, Taoke sent without prompting. *A kill and feeding. Your pack mates and many others have been here.*

Lynch tried "sending," directing his thought toward the dway. *Can you tell them apart?*

To his surprise, he was answered. *Yes. The prey was here.* That much was obvious, blood and gore still stained the floor. *The rest are unknown to me. There is one that I have sensed before. At my pack den.*

When, asked Syn, *during a show?*

Before the show, after the killings.

That narrows it down a bit, Syn thought to himself. *But not much.* Still, something about what Taoke sent tickled his mind.

Would you know these scents again? Lynch asked.

Of course.

They had gotten all they could from the Potee St. house. Again, they hustled Taoke into the wagon and they drove to the alley where the double slaying had taken place.

Higgins backed the wagon into the alley off Broadway. Lynch went ahead to keep anyone from coming the other way. Syn unlocked the wagon's back door, very conscious that there was nothing to stop Taoke if he decided to run away.

The dway did not. He was on the hunt and a dway does not leave the hunt until the prey has been brought down and even then, he does not leave his pack.

More killing, he sent. *Death here*, he indicated where Laverne Dixon had been killed. *And here.* Where Roy Conner had fallen. *And blood here.*

Taoke stood close to where the knife had been found. *Your beast's blood was shed. It is… human. And the same from the place we just left. I remember now. It is from the one who came after the killing. You stepped out. She came in and looked at me. She saw me, was happy, and left.*

Oh God no! Syn thought as he realized who the woman was. He hoped he was wrong. He hoped Taoke was wrong, although he knew the dway was not.

"Higgins, was Dr. Cruz ever on this scene?"

"No, why?"

"What about on Potee St.?"

"No. We called but she just sent the field people with instructions to examine, wrap, and bag. Why do you…" Jane Higgins was a very good detective. She quickly answered the question she was about to ask. Echoing Syn's thoughts, she said aloud, "Oh God no! You don't think…"

"It makes a weird kind of sense when you think about it." To the dway Syn sent, *Taoke, please get back into the wagon.*

Is the hunt over, Scarecrow?

Not yet, we still have to bring down the prey.

Syn called Lynch back to the wagon and told him what Taoke had found and what he suspected.

"That's crazy," the detective said.

"Lynch," answered Higgins, "think about this case. Think about what we've got in the back of the wagon. This case has been nothing but crazy. Remember, nobody but the Scarecrow here was even thinking monster until Dela Cruz came up with the idea."

"So, Syn, Higgins, what do we do next? Go to Fuller and tell him we've cracked the case based on the olfactory senses of the Big Bad Wolf? He'd never believe us."

"Fuller would," Syn said, "but he'd be the only one. We need something more."

"Like what?" Lynch demanded to know.

Syn shrugged. "Standard police procedure. We confront our suspect with the evidence and see what happens."

CHASTEL'S JOURNAL

The dreams are fading, as is the pleasure. The food that sustains them and me is running low. I will have to go out tonight. Younger people maybe, out for fun. I wonder if their flesh will be more tender.

Chapter Eighteen

Syn called the Medical Examiner's Office. At that time of night, only the field investigators were there.

"Another body, detective?" asked the FI on duty. "Hope it's not another Beast case."

"No, it's not, but it's in reference to the Beast. I need to speak with Dr. Cruz."

"She won't be in until tomorrow."

"I need to speak with her tonight. It's an emergency."

"I don't know what could be so important but okay, I'll call her from another line. Just hold on." Syn did. Ten minutes later the FI came back. "No answer. She usually answers so I guess she's out. Don't know where she'd be going this time of night though."

Syn did or thought he did. He said a quick "Thanks," hung up the pay phone, and went back to the wagon.

"She's out," he told Higgins and Lynch. "Maybe on the hunt."

"So, what do we do? Put out an APB on her saying she might be the Beast's next target?"

"No," Higgins replied. "That would get too many people involved." After a moment's thought she said. "I have an idea."

The idea led to her and Lynch riding in the back of the wagon, Syn driving, and Taoke crammed uncomfortably into the passenger seat. The dway had his head partially out of the lowered window, sniffing the air in the manner of his more primitive canine cousins.

Lynch knew Cruz's address. He had picked the ME up once or twice to take her to a crime scene. The plan was for Syn to drive to her house then begin circling until Taoke caught her scent. They were five blocks away when…

Go left, Taoke sent to him. Syn did, then followed the dway's directions as they followed a trail east and north away from her house.

Tommy Lister and Fay Stewart didn't care about the curfew. She was seventeen, he was a year older. They were young and thought they were in love. They had been dating for six months. They had kissed and necked and that was all but now they were ready.

That afternoon they had taken a walk in the park after school. There they found what they just knew was the perfect spot to fully express their love. They agreed to meet there after both their families were asleep.

It was not the first time they had snuck out. There were not many police patrols in their neighborhood and the cops were too busy to stop them. Anyway, they used backyards and the open spaces behind houses to their best advantage.

Soon they embraced in their secluded spot, well hidden by trees and bushes but somehow lit by the light of the gibbous moon.

It was by chance that The Beast had seen Tommy. She could have taken him at any time but suspected he was sneaking off to the park. Maybe to meet someone. The thought excited her. She followed.

We're heading to Gwynn's Park, Syn sent to Taoke. *Tell the others. Tell them to be ready.*

Arriving at the park, Syn turned onto South Gwynn Road and took the wagon as far as he could. Then he and Taoke got out. As he was unlocking the back door to let Higgin and Lynch out, Taoke growled and ran into the trees.

"Now what?" Lynch asked.

Syn drew his revolver. "We follow him."

They were down to panties and jockeys. *This is it,* Fay thought. She was more nervous than she had ever been. *Will it hurt? Will I be good for him? I hope he's not just using me.*

Tommy was nervous as well. *I hope I can get it in. I hope I last long enough for her. What if she gets pregnant?*

Despite his fears, Tommy smiled at Fay. "You ready? You sure?"

Despite her worries, Fay smiled back. "Yes, I'm sure. Let's do… it."

Their final pieces of clothing came off. She lay down, he moved toward her.

Then came the growl.

They were not yet one, but they turned as one and saw a clawed figure come toward them. Tommy pushed his love away. "Run," he said, then bravely but foolishly stood and put himself between beauty and Beast.

A clawed hand rose to strike. Then came another growl, a deeper one, a meaner one. Taoke fell on the Beast. Claws both natural and manufactured slashed and cut. Tommy heard a gunshot and a man's voice shouted, "Dammit, you fools, RUN!"

Leaving their clothes, Tommy and Fay did just that.

Taoke, back off. DO NOT KILL HER, Syn sent, hoping the dway would not give way to blood lust. *That would be hard to explain,* he thought to himself.

It was difficult for Taoke to pull away from his prey. But obeying the pack leader was in his nature and, for now, he was part of Scarecrow's pack. He stood, ignoring the minor wounds the Beast had inflicted.

Although deeper than those she had inflicted on Taoke, Dr. Dela Cruz's wounds were also minor. As she stood, she found herself surrounded by a snarling dwayyo and three detectives with their guns. She stood crouched, her claws extended, as if ready to attack.

"Why, Dela?" Syn asked.

Cruz gave them a crazy smile as she and the Beast inside her united. "It's in the blood, you know. My blood." She looked toward Taoke. "His blood. His blood is my blood, from long ago."

"Give it up, doctor," Lynch said. "You know this can only end one way."

"What, with me locked up in a cage? Put on exhibit like him. No, not that way."

She sprang from her crouch and rushed Higgins whom she believed was the weakest. *Get past her and I'll be free, free to find and kill the young ones I was denied.*

Dela Cruz was wrong about Jane Higgins. The detective showed no hesitation about firing her revolver again and again until it clicked empty. Lynch and Syn also fired, bringing the Beast down before she could move more than five steps.

Some distance away, the lovers held each other as they listened to the sounds of gunfire. They were scared, but in their fear was also excitement. "You saved me," Fay said. "You offered your life for me."

"What else could I do, Fay? I love you."

Fear and excitement mixed. They fell to the bare ground and finished what they had started earlier. And it was wonderful. Bonded by and lost in love, heedless of their state of undress, they went home and were together forever.

"So now what do we do?" asked Lynch looking down at Dela Cruz's body. "We've got a dead ME who was also the Beast and a dwayyo in the back of the wagon. No way we're going to be able to explain this."

"This is Harbor City," Syn replied. "Who says we'll have to?" *Taoke,* he sent, *you did well. But now you have to decide. Do you want to go back to the circus or rejoin your old pack?*

The dway did not hesitate. *One does not desert the pack. I will be the Big Bad Wolf.*

"Higgins, Lynch, put Taoke in the wagon and drive him back to York. Call Fuller on the way and tell him where to meet me."

"What about...?" Higgins pointed to the body.

"Don't worry about it. By tomorrow it will all be sorted."

And so, it was. When Fuller arrived in Gwynn Park, Syn told him everything, including Taoke's part in it. Together they came up with a story that did not include the dwayyo.

Since no one from the captain's office on up wanted the public to know that the Beast had really been one of the city's medical examiners, the same ME whose reports on her own victims had led to the Corbet Woods disaster, Fuller and Syn's story was mostly accepted, particularly since a search of Dr. Cruz's house turned up the Chastel journal and a few suspicious packages of meat. As a result, Mayor Gibson's press conference was short and to the point, with no questions asked.

"It is with deep sorrow that I announce the death of Dr. Dela Cruz at the hands of the Beast. It is believed that the Beast directly targeted Dr. Cruz in the mistaken belief that she was getting close to his identity. Detectives of the Homicide Unit learned of this and tried to contact Dr. Cruz but were too late to prevent her abduction. They tracked the pair to Gwynn Park where they found Dr. Cruz dead. When the Beast attacked them, they had no choice but to kill it. A sad ending to a sad chapter in Harbor City's history. And for those wondering, the body of the Beast was cremated without being identified. Let the very human monster remain forever nameless."

Epilogue

Some years later

Theodore Syn sat on the front porch of his rancher and looked up at the night sky. He and Cara had bought the house three years ago when it became difficult for her to climb stairs. A year later, she was in need of full-time care, so Syn resigned from the HCPD to be with her. She passed the following year, leaving Syn alone, his nephew Jericho having moved to Baltimore to join the BPD.

Syn thought about his life. He had done some good and made some mistakes. There had been happiness and sadness, magic and sorrow. He thanked God for his blessings, for Cara, for Jericho, and for his other family, the snallygasters, and now the dwayyo. The two had bonded, with the snallys hunting with the dway and the dwayyo sharing their essence with the snallys. Thinking of this, Syn shuddered at what the resultant chicks might be like. Still, Syn had decided, it would not do to leave them alone, unguarded and unprotected.

Which is why he had called in a favor from on high to be appointed as a ranger in the South Mountain State Park in western Frederick County. There he would be able to keep watch over both flock and pack.

He could see the mountains from his porch. *Tomorrow*, he thought, *I'll be part of you. Maybe I always have been, ever since Kona embraced me and drew out my essence, ever since I fought against the dway and later hunted with one.*

It was late. Packed and ready to go, he had spent the entire night on the porch, just thinking and remembering. He looked at his watch and again he looked at the mountains. *I belong there more than here.*

Daylight comes, he thought. *I want to go home.*

About the Author

John L. French is a retired crime scene supervisor with forty years' experience. He has seen more than his share of murders, shootings, and serious assaults. As a break from the realities of his job, he started writing science fiction, pulp, horror, fantasy, and, of course, crime fiction.

John's first story "Past Sins" was published in Hardboiled Magazine and was cited as one of the best Hardboiled stories of 1993. More crime fiction followed, appearing in Alfred Hitchcock's Mystery Magazine, the Fading Shadows magazines and in collections by Barnes and Noble. Association with writers like James Chambers and the late, great C.J. Henderson led him to try horror fiction and to a still growing fascination with zombies and other undead things. His first horror story "The Right Solution" appeared in Marietta Publishing's *Lin Carter's Anton Zarnak*. Other horror stories followed in anthologies such as *The Dead Walk* and *Dark Furies*, both published by Die Monster Die books. It was in *Dark Furies* that his character Bianca Jones made her literary debut in "21 Doors," a story based on an old Baltimore legend and a creepy game his daughter used to play with her friends.

John's first book was *The Devil of Harbor City*, a novel done in the old pulp style. *Past Sins* and *Here There Be Monsters* followed. John was also consulting editor for Chelsea House's *Criminal Investigation* series. His other books include *The Assassins' Ball* (written with Patrick Thomas), *Souls on Fire*, *The Nightmare Strikes*, *Monsters Among Us*, *The Last Redhead*, the *Magic of Simon Tombs*, *The Santa Heist* (written with Patrick Thomas), *When the Moon Shines*, and *Mortal Sins*. John is the editor of *To Hell in a Fast Car*, *Mermaids 13*, C. J. Henderson's *Challenge of the Unknown*, *Camelot 13* (with Patrick Thomas), *With Great Power...* (with Greg Schauer) and *Devilish and Divine* (with Danielle Ackley-McPhail).

You can find John on Facebook or you can email him at him at jfrenchfam@aol.com.

artist's rendition of the Dwayyo

DWAYYO

(Also known as Dewayo, Hexenwolf, Snarly Yow)

ORIGINS: Accounts of this cryptid first appear in Frederick County dating back as early as the 1920's and '30's, but could date back as far as the 1700s, believed by some to be related to the Dutch hexenwolf. German settlers of the region counted the dwayyo as protection against the snallygasters, their natural enemy, thus the paint or hanging of hex signs on buildings in the community to this day. Other accounts cite them as the earliest occurrence of dogmen.

DESCRIPTION: These are bipedal creatures ranging in height from four to eight feet tall or more. Some accounts cite them as the size of a deer, others, the size of a bear. There have been reports of them running on all fours, but their general stance is noted as upright. They have canine or wolf-like features and bushy tails and long hair. Their coats can be a range of colors, from black, dark brown, grey, fawn, or brindle, sometimes with stripes on their lower section. Some reports note powerful legs, muscular like a kangaroo. Their cries are most described as growling like a wolf or a dog, or horrid screams.

LIFE CYCLE: Little is known about the life expectancy of dwayyo, or the stages of their life. It is known that they are pack animals. They are photo-phobic and avoid bright light and thus are usually nocturnal hunters.

HISTORY: As early as the 18th century, there have been accounts of bipedal wolf-like creatures in Frederick County, in particular the areas of West Middleton and Wolfsville.

The first mention specifically attributed to dwayyo is from 1944, and is limited to frightful screams and footprints in West Middleton. The period of greatest activity and reported first-hand encounters occurred in the 1960s and 70s, near Gambrill State Park, Route 77, and Cunningham Falls State Park.

In December 1965, around 100 local college students signed up to hunt the dwayyo, but none of them showed up at the scheduled time. There continue to be reported sightings as recently as 2020, though some claim the dwayyo have shifted their territory closer to Port Deposit and the Conowing Dam.

artist's rendition of the Beast of Gevaudan

THE BEAST OF GEVAUDAN

ORIGINS: Said to be active between 1764 and 1767 in the region Gevaudan, France, there were many theories as to the nature of the beast, purported to be a were-wolf, a shape-shifting sorcerer, or a somehow surviving prehistoric beast. Dedicated hunts are said to have ended the beast's reign of terror, but agreement as to the nature of the creature or creatures have never been reached. It is believed there was likely at minimum a breading pair, and perhaps young.

Description: Accounts of the beast vary wildly, enough so that sources agree there must have been more than one, despite the cryptid's name. It is a vicious creature said to move on all fours, roughly the size of a cow or horse. The coloring is reported as either solid red, or red with a grey patch or strips down the back, though some accounts describe it as not being red at all, rather with black and white patches all over. Witnesses claimed it had the features of a bear, wolf, hyena, and panther all at once, with small round ears close to the head and a long snout lined with large teeth. It was said to have a long, strong neck, and an equally long and strong tufted tail, which it used whip-like to attack its prey. It was known to ambush its prey, seizing it by the neck and even decapitating its victims. Accounts depict it with either split hooves or hoof-like tips to each toe, while others posited that the creature's claws were simply heavy and thick enough to resemble hooves. The other distinctive feature cited is that the beast was believed to be impervious to normal bullets.

Given the length of time since these documented attacks, written accounts are all we can go on. Based on those, however, crypto-zoologists theorize the beast was either a new variant or a hybrid of existing animals, or a prehistoric species such as a Bear-dog, Dire Wolf, or Hyaenodon, that somehow survived unnoticed. Another theory is that the creature could potentially be a member of an extinct group of hooved predators called mesonychids, based on even earlier accounts from the regions of Armenia and Assyria.

LIFE CYCLE: Unknown, although some accounts document a mated pair traveling with grown young.

HISTORY: Over the three years of documented attacks allegedly by the Beast of Gevaudan, nearly one hundred deaths are attributed to the creature, along with a number of unsuccessful attacks.

Primarily known for attacking solitary people, mostly but not exclusively women and children, there are accounts of the beast attacking and being driven off by groups.

One such attack upon a group of children, successfully repelled by ten-year-old Jacques Portefaix, resulted in the boy being given a bounty by the King and an education paid for by the crown. At one point there was a 6,000-livre bounty on the creature's head, resulting in many attempts to hunt it. The attacks went on for two more years, though several creatures believed to be the beast were killed over that time. In June of 1767 Jean Chastel was reported to have shot a wolf-like creature with a silver bullet. The stomach of the slain beast contained human remains and the creature had characteristics not found in wolves. No clear identification was made of the beast's nature, but the killings did cease, giving credence to the fact that was the beast.

Although Jason Whitley has worn many creative hats, he is at heart a traditional illustrator and painter. With author James Chambers, Jason collaborates and illustrates the sometimes-prose, sometimes graphic novel, *The Midnight Hour,* which is being collected into one volume by eSpec Books. His and Scott Eckelaert's newspaper comic strip, Sea Urchins, has been collected into four volumes. Along with eSpec Books' Systema Paradoxa series, Jason is working on a crime noir graphic novel. His portrait of Charlotte Hawkins Brown is on display in the Charlotte Hawkins Brown Museum.

CAPTURE THE CRYPTIDS!

Cryptid Crate is a monthly subscription box filled with various cryptozoology and paranormal themed items to wear, display and collect. Expect a carefully curated box filled with creeptastic pieces from indie makers and artisans pertaining to bigfoot, sasquatch, UFOs, ghosts, and other cryptid and mysterious creatures (apparel, decor, media, etc).

http://CryptidCrate.com